NO LONGER PROPERTY OF
SEATTLE PUBLIC LIBRARY

D0700161

BROADVIEW LIBRARY

THE HAPPY MAN

ERIC C. HIGGS was born in Sarasota, Florida, but raised throughout the United States, Japan and Europe, his father being a career Army officer. Eric's early education was received in such diverse venues as a small military schoolhouse in Okinawa and a boarding school in Switzerland.

After graduating from the University of Georgia, Eric worked as a general assignment reporter for the *Aiken Standard & Review*, Aiken, South Carolina, and then enlisted in the Navy. Eric served throughout the Pacific during his active duty Navy days and became qualified as a Surface Warfare Officer and Combatant Craft Officer-in-Charge.

Eric then affiliated with the Naval Reserve, and worked full time in the aerospace industry, first for General Dynamics and then Lockheed. It was during this time that Eric wrote and published *PT Commander* (Zebra Books), *Doppelganger* (St. Martin's Press) and *The Happy Man* (St. Martin's Press). Eric is a member of the Writers Guild of America (West).

Eric also realized his long-term goal of launching a full-time freelance writing business, specializing in proposals; business plans; résumés; technical documents; various types of marketing materials; and industrial video scripts.

As a Naval Reservist, Eric served in a variety of positions in the special warfare community, eventually being named as the Reserve Commanding Officer of Special Boat Unit Thirteen. Eric retired from the Reserves with the rank of Commander.

Eric and his wife Elaine recently celebrated their forty-second wedding anniversary. They have three grown children, and reside in Imperial Beach, California, where Eric is, as ever, sublimely happy.

ERIC C. HIGGS

THE HAPPY MAN

VALANCOURT BOOKS

The Happy Man by Eric C. Higgs
First published by St. Martin's Press in 1985
First Valancourt Books edition 2017

Copyright © 1985 by Eric C. Higgs
Introduction copyright © 2017 by Eric C. Higgs

All rights reserved. In accordance with the U.S. Copyright Act of 1976, the copying, scanning, uploading, and/or electronic sharing of any part of this book without the permission of the publisher constitutes unlawful piracy and theft of the author's intellectual property. If you would like to use material from the book (other than for review purposes), prior written permission must be obtained by contacting the publisher.

Published by Valancourt Books, Richmond, Virginia
http://www.valancourtbooks.com

ISBN 978-1-943910-94-6 (trade paperback)
ISBN 978-1-943910-95-3 (hardcover)
Also available as an electronic book.

All Valancourt Books publications are printed on acid free paper that meets all ANSI standards for archival quality paper.

Set in Dante MT
Cover by Henry Petrides

INTRODUCTION

THE MOST SURPRISING THING IN HAVING *The Happy Man* republished thirty years on is how it equals the excitement and freshness of its first publication. I'd like to think it's because a good story well told will stand the test of time. But mostly I believe it's because the secret lives of the normal-seeming, everyday middle class contain an unspeakable darkness that always fascinates, if one cares to dig deeply enough.

My own digging began shortly after I decided to settle in Southern California. I was in thrall to the abundant sunshine, wide-open landscapes and ever-widening circle of friends who were cheerfully shouldering their way into dazzling futures. Indeed, 'twas the smiling, sunglass-wearing California that had been as advertised in books and TV and the movies, and not at all disappointing.

And yet . . . there is always a fly in the ointment, a burr under the saddle blanket. People stubbornly remained people, oblivious to the wonderful stage set that had been prepared for them, and when the young engineer or lawyer or executive would lean close at a backyard pool party where tiki torches cast their wavering glow and the liquor or marijuana had finally taken hold, sometimes they'd say the most dreadful and darkly surprising of things.

What, I wondered as cast about for story ideas, would it be like to take these dark whisperings to the extreme? To write a story about some human demon dropped into the midst of this sunshine-drenched paradise? About a young software engineer, say, married to a beautiful woman and living in a prosperous upper-middle-class development . . . and who is suddenly beguiled by the monster who moved in next door. The story came to me rapidly, as I wish all writing would.

The critical reception to *The Happy Man* was largely positive and this was immensely gratifying, but the movie interest was bewitching. I learned how to write screenplays and talk to studio people, became a member of the Writers Guild, and found the door opening to many other opportunities, and while this led to sales to such organizations as Warner Bros. and HBO, none of these have (so far) come to fruition. But *The Happy Man* has remained under option to one various entity after another to this day, and it was in July of this year that the current option-holder conducted a full-on "table reading" of the screen adaptation, with all actors in place and hope, as ever in Los Angeles, springing eternal.

All this has been wonderful but my one regret is how I've neglected my novel writing over the pursuit of various movie and TV opportunities. I've only written two novels since then (*Doppelganger*, published by St. Martin's Press, and *PT Commander*, published by Zebra Books) although now I've recently returned to novel writing full time and have completed a first draft on a planned series of detective novels.

But that is for the future. This is now, and if you like a good combination of adventure, mystery, horror and intrigue . . . then please turn the page.

Eric C. Higgs
October 2017

for Elaine

One's cruelty is one's power; and when one parts with one's cruelty, one parts with one's power; and when one has parted with that, I fancy one's old and ugly.

The Way of the World
—William Congreve

One

The Marshes rotted in their house two full days before they were discovered by a deliveryman from Sparklett's.

He had been giving the doorbell its third and final buzz when he noticed a certain odor. As he would later tell a reporter, it was a smell he had become acquainted with in Vietnam. He put the plastic jug down and went around back, looking for a way to get in. At the rear of the house, facing the Jacuzzi deck, the big sliding glass door was wide open. The smell was so strong he had to clap a hand to his mouth.

He lost his breakfast shortly thereafter, although he neglected to mention this to the reporter. But I saw it happen. I saw him stagger backward until he fell from the Jacuzzi deck and into the bushes, which is where he gasped and retched. I observed the scene from my breakfast nook, masked by the partially open Levolors.

By late afternoon the property was roped off. Two police cars were parked out front, light bars pulsing with yellow warning beacons, amplified radios squawking loud enough to be heard two blocks away. A beige panel truck was backed into the drive-way, the black lettering on the door of which read CORONER. A brightly painted Action News van had its side doors swung open, and I could see a technician inside adjusting a knob underneath some kind of oscilloscope. The van's double-pronged trans-mitter was ratcheted to the limit of its telescopic pole, pointing back toward town.

A dozen or so neighbors were gathered around the spectacle, whispering to each other, shaking their heads, passing the latest rumor. Housewives mostly, but also a few men and a scattering of some quiet, solemn children. Everyone was there who had a reason to be home at this hour of the afternoon.

Except, of course, for me. I chose to stay inside, even though the Marsh house was right next door.

I watched a young woman in a business suit talking with a wide-shouldered cop. Next to her a slender guy in jeans chewed gum impassively, a Minicam casually balanced on his shoulder. The deliveryman stood in the background, a pained expression on his handsome, weather-beaten face. The cop walked away from the woman, shaking his head in what looked like an obvious "no comment." The young woman looked at her watch and said something to the cameraman. He swung the lens down and squinted into the eyepiece. She straightened her shoulders and brought the microphone to chin level.

I looked at the little portable on the breakfast counter, which was tuned to the same channel. The gray-haired anchorman said it was time to go to a live remote from Mesa Vista Estates, and then the girl was on—looking, I thought, a little plumper than in real life. She scowled like a Methodist deacon as she gave a brief rundown on what she knew about the murders, which was just about nothing, and as she spoke she slowly eased her way toward the deliveryman. When he was finally in the camera's field of view, she thrust the microphone at him so abruptly he recoiled. The name patch on his workshirt read *Pete*.

I took another sip from the half-full tumbler of bourbon, grimacing at the taste.

"... then I called the police soon as I could," the deliveryman was saying. "Let me tell you, once you smell something like that you don't ever forget it. Back in 'Nam, me and this corporal had to go down this tunnel we fragged 'cause you always had to count the VC bodies, and lady, that is just about the way it smelled back of these poor folks' house...."

Then something interesting happened, a bit of providence I imagine cameramen pray for. The first of the covered stretchers came out, and the picture on the little television wobbled as he cut away from the deliveryman and hurried over. Just as he panned down for a close shot, the corpse's arm slipped from underneath the white sheet.

The stretcher bearers must have been flustered, for rather than stopping to tidy things up they started a mad little dash for their truck, anxious to get away from the cameraman. The television showed the hand dragging along the grass, utterly slack, skittering as the knuckles caught and bounced across the carefully tended lawn.

About an hour later there was a knock at the door. It was a mustachioed young man who looked a bit like Joe Namath in his heyday, and he introduced himself as Sergeant Hernron of the Chula Vista Police Department. He took out a notepad and asked if I wouldn't mind answering a few questions. Hear anything last night? Night before? How well did I know the Marshes? Had Mr. Marsh spoken of any threats he had received, anything of that nature? I shook my head to all his questions. He put the notebook back and said he'd be in touch if there were further questions. I put my hand on the rough, doubleknit texture of his sleeve and asked exactly what had happened.

"Bud, you don't wanna know."

I followed the news carefully, and the favored theory had it that it was a burglary gone awry, probably at the hands of illegal aliens. It was pointed out that the little development of Mesa Vista was only three miles from the Mexican border, and in the past there had been robberies by illegals.

But that was it. Things died down, and within days the Marsh affair was supplanted by SWAT TEAM NAILS FREEWAY SNIPER and FATHER OF FOUR RUNS AMOK.

But I kept watch over the Marsh place, especially at night. Just me and my old friend Mr. Jack Daniels. I stared at their windows, not even knowing what I was looking for. I half expected to see the disembodied face of Ruskin Marsh himself—looming, perhaps, in the bay window, a spectre condemned to walk the split-level living/dining area until the House of Marsh fell asunder. Which, considering how hastily thrown together Mesa Vista was, might be only ten years' worth of chain rattling.

But nothing ever happened. Even so, I could not give up the watch. As the days passed into weeks, I began to look on it as a kind of job, which went some way toward assuaging my conscience. It made me feel better about being fired. Now, if I could only find something to make me feel good about the fact that I'm stone-broke, well . . . or that my wife has gone . . . or that I'm going into the fourth month of not meeting the mortgage payment . . . or that the little Mazda RX-7 is already on the lot at Honest John's Repo Depo . . .

So I rambled around the old homestead, unshaven, looking out the side window and thinking and waiting and talking out loud to no one. And the Marsh place sat there, a plain lump of white stucco giving off no more evil than a Barbie dollhouse, its only glow the Southern California sunshine refracting off its energy-efficient windows. Nothing there, not any more than any other house in this development. I thought about that and laughter came from my throat, unbidden. It was a dry, rustling, witless sound.

Sometimes I would think back to the times Ruskin Marsh and I used to talk. I would think about the things he had hinted at, things that were so monstrous on the face of it that I never dreamed he might be in deadly earnest. But he was. Oh yes . . .

And I would close my eyes tight and grip hard on the Black Jack and my psyche would slide apart as if my brain were a freshly cut grapefruit, the disconnected halves falling from each other and rocking on their skins.

. . . a visitor came, and he wasn't on a foreclosure errand from the Bank of America. He was elderly and tall and thin, neat but far from dour. Clothes perhaps a shade too stylish for a man his age. His eyes were startlingly clear, the pupils black pinpricks in a field of gray.

"Excuse me, sir." He doffed his snap-brim hat. "I'm from Techlydyne's main office in San Francisco."

Techlydyne was the outfit Ruskin had worked for. The breath in my lungs dropped twenty degrees.

"Are you here about the Marshes?" I held the door half-open, partly to hide the fact that I was in an unwashed kimono at four in the afternoon, standard uniform for unemployed jack-offs.

"Yes, that's exactly why I'm here." His face muscles worked to reveal his incisors. "To investigate this terrible tragedy. Company insurance policy . . ." He waved his hat as the words trailed off. ". . . You know."

"Well, then." I opened the door wide, no longer concerned about looking like a bum. This guy wouldn't care about that, not if he was who I thought he was. "Please come in."

He stepped out of the blinding sun—must have been roasting in that dark suit, poor devil—and into my shadowy lair. The only sound was the central air, on high and hissing gently. Even the television was off. We walked down the short corridor, cluttered with dirty clothes where I had dropped them, and into the living room. "Please have a seat," I said calmly, masking the speed with which my heart was beginning to race.

He walked to the camelback sofa and swept the old newspapers to the floor, as if it were a perfectly natural thing to do. He sat, putting his alligator-hide briefcase across his lap. Snap of the brass latches. Withdrew a yellow legal pad. His hands were long and graceful, not at all like an old man's hands. I watched one slip into his inside pocket and produce a long, silvery pen; a Mont Blanc, I believe. He offered an urbane, apologetic smile. "Do you mind if I take notes? My memory is like a sieve."

"Of course not."

A grin that Charlton Heston would have envied. "Fine." Raise of an eyebrow, Mont Blanc poised over the pad. "I take it then you're Charles Ripley?"

So he knew my name. Of course he would. "That's right. Did Ruskin speak of me?"

Now his eyes joined in on the grin, positively glistening with merriment. "Yes. He wrote about you."

I grinned back as I eagerly leaned forward. "Then you're not really from Techlydyne, are you?"

No change of that happy expression. Just a slow nod. Right, Mr. Ripley, his gray eyes seemed to be saying. You guessed who I was right off the bat. Now we can drop all pretense, can't we?

It was as if I'd been puzzling over an abstract painting and the sense of it had come through in sudden focus. I knew now what I had to do. And not only for this day, but for all the tomorrows I might have left. The design stretched before me in terms so simple and precise I had to wonder that it had taken this old man's visit to make it thus. My insides thrummed with fierce excitement.

I got up and went toward him, forcing myself to smile.
The monster smiled back.

It was only three steps from the laundry room to the garage
but it was still risky carrying the old man across the open walkway. It was broad daylight, and the houses here were quite close.

I made it inside the darkness of the two-car garage—empty
save for the old man's Budget Rent-a-Car Fairlane, which I had
backed in earlier—and hefted the body from my shoulder and
down into the trunk. I pushed on the lid and it slammed shut with
a cheap, tinny *thunk*.

I went back into the house, grimly determined to finish the
rest of this day as if I were a machine, running through my depar-
ture checklist as quickly as possible.

But the blood on the kitchen floor gave me pause. Dear lord,
so much, so very much . . .

It hadn't gone as I had planned. I had approached the old man
in a kind of trance, confident that his death was as preordained
as the orbit of the solar system. But as soon as I put my hands
around his throat he exploded into frenzied activity, grabbing my
arms and snarling and trying to get his knee up into my groin.
That brought me to the here and now, and I threw myself into the
struggle as if I were fighting a much younger man.

He was in surprisingly good shape, and did not waste any
energy crying out for help. His own hands eventually found their
way to my throat, and his grip was like a steel vise. We stumbled
around the house, locked to each other throat to throat, his face
a horrible contortion of desperate rage. But I was stronger, and
eventually maneuvered the fight toward the utility closet, and
once there used one hand to yank the toolbox from its shelf. Its
contents spilled to the floor, and the first thing that came to hand
was a three-pound ball peen hammer.

He was still upright after the first blow, and I watched him
stagger toward the kitchen with his hands clasped to his skull.
He made an awful kind of gasping noise, as if he were choking.
Blood poured thickly from his scalp, covering his hands and spilling onto the padded shoulders of his jacket. He hit against the
dishwasher and rebounded away, stumbling like a drunk, and

some of the blood started hitting the floor in dark little splatters

For a moment I was frozen, stunned by the spectacle. Now that he was a distance away, he looked like any old gentleman who had been victimized by some terrible accident. But I reminded myself of who he was and what he had done, and the anger quickly rekindled. As I rushed upon him I told myself there could be no pity, not for his kind, not ever. And when I knocked him over and got on top of him, I brought the hammer down so hard and so often I was entirely unaware that I was making it end too quickly.

But now, as I surveyed the kitchen, I wondered if I could discharge the greater plan with the cool rationality it required—and not rely upon the rage that had propelled me through this act. Otherwise there might be mistakes. And failure.

I shook it off, like a wet dog ridding itself of water, and thought of the many things yet to do. I ran some water in a pail, and gathered up some likely looking cleaning wonders. I got on my knees and went to work, scrubbing. It was an onerous chore, but at least the floor was stain-resistant Congoleum.

My confidence slowly returned. There was even a little tingling of anticipation. The inertia that had once held me was indeed gone.

Then I shaved, or rather, I hacked away at what was rapidly becoming a beard. I got dressed—pastel knit shirt with an animal on the pocket, Calvin Klein jeans—gathered a few more things, including the old man's alligator briefcase, and threw them in a battered suitcase that had served me since college. Then I put on a white jacket of a rough grade of silk, one I had picked up a long, long time ago in Hong Kong.

Check in the mirror. Looking out was your standard All-American lean-and-clean boy. Mr. Junior Chamber of Commerce, California style. Except for the eyes, which weren't exactly right, somehow. They seemed too wide, perhaps even a little too bright. But other than that I was looking at a reasonable facsimile of what I had once been. I tried a test smile but could not find the right strings. Strange I could no longer force even that; in the past they had been so easy to fake. I straightened the collar on my jacket.

I grabbed the suitcase handle and went into the living room. I went around the house and shut all the blinds, then turned on some but not all of the lights. As if Shelly were still with me, and I doing nothing more than setting up the house before we would go out for a dinner or a movie. There was a stinging in my eyes, and I tried to swing my mind elsewhere, chanting *keep moving, get going, be a machine*.

I went out through the laundry room and pulled the door shut, twisting the knob to make sure it was locked. It was unlikely They would report the old man's absence to the police. And it would be days, if not weeks, before They sent someone else to check me out.

But by then . . .

I got into the Fairlane and buckled the seatbelt. The engine started on the first go and I was down the driveway, automatic garage door closing behind me for the last time.

I drove through the winding streets of the development, seeing few people among the jumble of closely set homes. I drove by the marker that proclaimed MESA VISTA ESTATES—it too was made of stucco, and even had its own little tile roof—and turned onto the main road.

I brought the Ford up to speed and headed west on the new four-lane. The land was open and undeveloped on either side— gently rolling hills of chaparral thicketed with scrub, clumped shrubbery, and huge boulders.

Five minutes later I was in Chula Vista, the municipality at San Diego's southern edge. Perhaps I might have lived here one day, after a suitable promotion. There had once been talk of my stepping into a project manager's slot, a thousand years ago.

After ten minutes of school zones and stoplights I was on Interstate 5 heading north. The tall, chunky buildings of downtown San Diego lay dead ahead, not looking much different than St. Louis or Denver or any other midsized burg. Only the complex freeway interchanges and nearness of the Pacific let me know I was in California.

The interstate curved around the bland hunk of buildings that was the city's center. I saw the exit where I used to get off to go to work, and part of me wanted to go down that off-ramp,

follow the next familiar series of turns and stops, and go inside
the skyscraper of mirrored glass and ride the elevator to the floor
Aerotel leased and walk across the bullpen to my old office and sit
at my desk and reach into the In basket and start the day of work.

But I stared straight ahead as I whipped by the exit, and tried
not to think that I would never use it again, nor indeed ever see
this city again. Ten years I had lived here, and had grown from
boy to man, from single to married, from liberal arts aesthete to
aerospace engineer.

I gripped the wheel hard as I looked in the rearview mirror,
taking in my last glimpse. And wondered if things might have
somehow come out different.

Two

If it hadn't been a fine summer, neither had it been particularly bad. Just bland. But then, I was long past the time when summer was a big event. No more midnight beach bonfires, no more lazy days of sailing, not for this hardworking kid. These days, when I wasn't busting my ass at Aerotel I was busting my ass in our tiny yard, which was what I was doing the Saturday I met the Marshes.

A big Allied moving van had pulled up the previous day and discharged a household. Shelly and I caught brief glimpses of the new arrivals—a man, a woman, a boy, and a cat—and we talked of dropping by when they got settled in. There was no organized Welcome Wagon in our little community; Mesa Vista Estates, only four years old, had not reached that point of neighborhood organization. But everyone was beginning to recognize everyone else, and there were occasional parties. The sense of neighborhood was slowly growing, like the shrubs and trees the developer had laid down, now only half-grown.

Saturday I attended to my mowing chores. The edge of my backyard gave onto a small valley about one hundred yards deep. It was covered with pale, wispy scrub, dotted with an occasional green bush. On the other side of the valley, about a quarter-mile distant, another housing development was perched atop the ridge. Viewscape Estates, I believe it was called. To the south there was absolutely nothing, just gently rolling, almost barren hills giving onto the tractless wastes of Mexico. This view had added an extra two thousand dollars to the price of the house—ours was the basic "Matador" model, although the only Mexican thing about it so far as I knew was the tile roof—and two years ago, when we had bought it, the view seemed worthwhile. Now I no longer noticed it.

I moved the electric mower over the brief bits of lawn that constituted our backyard, the mower's long orange cord trailing behind. The backyard was so small about all I could do was circle the Jacuzzi deck, then weave around the clumps of bushes that had come with the house. Suddenly the mower went dead, and as I knelt to reconnect the plug I saw the new neighbor lady looking at me.

She was behind the sliding glass door of their living room, about thirty yards away. She smiled and opened the door, came walking toward the waist-high wooden fence that separated our backyards. I got up and walked over, wiping my hands, smiling a neighborly smile.

My first impression was that this was a woman who could make her living advertising athletic equipment. She shone with the good looks that are worshipped out here—lustrous blond hair, knockout figure, glowing health.

But, as we drew nearer, I saw that this was not your standard vibrant matron. No, for that you had to look at someone like my wife Shelly. Or at least a picture of what she had looked like eight years ago, when I first met her. This new neighbor lady was different. Her face had the exotic bone structure of a fashion model out of *Vogue*. Her hair splayed wide in soft, frizzy curls. She was very fair, the type who reddens but never browns. She wore a tight Danskin top and carefully faded cutoffs. She was about thirty, I guessed. I became conscious that my smile was no longer neighborly but kind of ridiculous and pasted on, like the self-conscious mask I wore when I made my first bashful but eager attempts at asking out girls.

"Hello, there." Her voice was deep and silky.

"Welcome to Mesa Vista. I'm Charles Ripley, next-door neighbor."

"Sybil Marsh." We shook briefly, then she slid her fingers into the jean's pockets. It was a tight fit, enough so that she had to worm her hands in there, making her breasts sort of press against the black, sheer material . . .

"You probably saw us moving in yesterday."

I nodded. "Sure did. Are you all new to San Diego?"

"Yes, we just moved down from San Francisco. My husband's company transferred him here."

"San Francisco's an awfully pretty city. I hope it's not a letdown coming here."

"Oh, no. Not at all. We were all ready for a change. I think it's quite lovely."

She smiled and looked at me frankly. It's been said that when people of the opposite sex first meet, they size each other up as possible bed partners. But that was not the way this woman regarded me. It was as if she were in an art gallery looking at something only mildly interesting. Her gray eyes, beautiful as they were, conveyed no shining intelligence.

For myself, I guess I glowed with standard masculine interest. Not that I was on the lookout for extramarital flings, no sir, but, well, this Sybil woman was definitely a welcome addition to the neighborhood. I became conscious of the silence. "Know it's always a trying time when you first move in."

"I think it'll be years before we get properly settled. I'm about ready to say the hell with it, let's just use those big cardboard boxes for furniture."

We laughed, as if it were a good joke.

"I was taking a break from all that unpacking when I saw you working in your yard."

"Well, my wife and I were planning to drop by sometime and roll out the welcome mat."

She held up a hand. "Please. The place is a jungle. I don't believe it'll ever get straight."

"Then why don't you and your husband come over tonight for a drink?"

She nodded slowly. "All right. Fine. What time should we come?"

I shrugged, smiled. "Eight."

A little boy came running from the house. He looked to be eight or nine, and he had a mop of jet black hair. He ran to Sybil and tugged at one of her back pockets. "Dad says for you to come help with the pictures." He was panting, almost breathless. "He says I'm not tall enough."

"All right, Mark." Sybil ruffled his hair. "But first I want you to meet Mr. Ripley. He's our new next-door neighbor."

He extended his hand, grinning. Standard kid, but somehow he managed to project an air of precocious worldliness. A lot of kids seem to do that these days.

"Hello, young man."

His was a hard, clamping grip. "Pleased to meet you, Mr. Ripley. I hope you're as nice as our last neighbor."

"I hope so, too."

He released me and turned to his mother. "Remember Mr. Hazard? He was just about the best neighbor anyone could have."

She chuckled as she gave his hair one last affectionate ruffle. "He certainly was. Now scoot."

Mark ran back to the house. I watched him bound up the Jacuzzi deck and wondered, as I cannot help myself from doing whenever I see other people's kids, what it would be like to have one of my own. Shelly had been pregnant two years ago, but the child was stillborn. Her doctor had told her she shouldn't try again, unfortunately. We were still talking about adoption, though less and less of late, it seemed.

"Well, see you tonight, Charles."

"Yeah, sure." I bobbed my head eagerly. "Nice to have met you."

She turned and walked to her house. Just as she stepped onto the raised patio, she glanced back in time to catch my eyes glued to her gracefully rolling hips. She gave a little good-bye wave, the fingers wiggling like a bunch of tiny snakes.

Shelly was pleased with the news. She immediately opened *The Joy of Cooking* and concentrated on preparing an elaborate tray of hors d'oeuvres. I was dispatched to the supermarket with instructions to supplement our alcohol larder with something other than white wine. Also—as long as I was going anyway—I was handed a list of small things to pick up, little jars of this and that from the gourmet section.

I strolled the aisles of the local Big Bear, my heart light and a whistle on my lips. The store was populated with its usual percentage of attractive women, and I could not help but notice that none of them held a candle to Sybil Marsh. I summoned the image of her sliding her hands into those tight little cutoffs . . . and shook my head wistfully. My new next-door neighbor.

Had I been twenty-two instead of thirty-two, I would've already prepared several likely stratagems that would have landed her in my sack. But those yeasty days were over and done. I no longer felt an urge to bed every woman I met, even one as delectable as Mrs. Marsh. And I was certain of my virtue, for when one nubile secretary or another would signal her availability for an office romance, I would primly decline. I was a straight arrow. Or, if truth be told, maybe only slightly bent. Once, while I was still in the Navy and Shelly and I had been married only a year, I fell just a little from the straight and narrow. It was in Olongapo, the shantytown just outside the Subic Bay Naval Station in the Philippines. I had gone to a party where, shortly after sitting down, I found myself being gobbled from underneath the table by a very young prostitute. It was sort of a party favor, you see. Back then a blow job cost exactly twenty-five cents, and the host had arranged for all guests to be serviced. Afterward, I didn't think about it much. There seemed to be no reason to get racked up over something that had only cost a quarter, after all.

I stocked up on hard booze, selecting the nationally known brands instead of the junk with the grocery store label. I got the little tins and jars of foreign stuff. A big bag of ice. Mixers.

I drove the RX-7 home a tad over the limit, enjoying the way its powerful little engine grabbed speed. Shelly was putting away the vacuum cleaner when I opened the front door. There was no time to make anything, so she heated up frozen dinners.

We ate the tasteless food as we watched the news on the counter-top Sony, the highlight of which was a fortyish woman on trial for murder. She had killed one of her young children with a shotgun. Her other kid had managed to scramble out the window.

I remembered the Minicam shots of her being led away by the police, back when the story first broke. It was in some neighborhood that was a little nicer than ours, and the woman looked exactly like any other middle-aged neighbor lady. Except, of course, for the handcuffs and this blank, empty look in her eyes.

Now the verdict was handed down, and it was innocent by reason of insanity. So far as I'd followed the trial, I had no argument with that. Then Shelly was up and the Osterizer was whirring with the last-minute preparations of her famous guacamole dip. I threw my aluminum tray in the trash and glanced through a handy bar guide I'd picked up at the supermarket, refreshing my memory as to the formulas for the more complicated drinks.

By eight I was ready for the front doorbell to ring, and so was surprised by the rapping at the sliding glass door that gave onto our Jacuzzi and miniature backyard. I turned and saw Sybil and the tall shape of her husband silhouetted against the twilight. I grinned hello as I walked across the living room, glad they hadn't caught me picking my nose. The door was unlocked, and Sybil's husband had already begun to slide it open.

"Hello, folks." I extended my hand and Mr. Marsh gave me a strong, solid grip. He was tall, something over six feet, with black hair like his son.

"Ruskin," Sybil said, "this is Charles Ripley, the man I was telling you about."

He gave another brisk shake, then let go. "Pleased to meet you."

"This way, folks."

I ushered them into the living room, Shelly meeting us at the midpoint. I made introductions in the same jolly tone I used at business luncheons. Sybil, I was pleased to note, wore the same Danskin top, but in deference to the evening had on long designer jeans. Ruskin Marsh looked like a hundred other guys I'd known and worked with. He was the Aggressive Exec type: smart, in good shape, with a slight undercurrent of ruthlessness.

I took drink orders and went off to the kitchen. Ruskin wanted a daiquiri and Sybil said that would be fine, so I decided to make it four.

When I came back, they were sitting around the coffee table, sampling the big tray of hors d'oeuvres.

"So tell us all about the neighborhood," Ruskin said. "The real estate agent was kind of vague."

"Mostly people our age," I replied. "Management-type guys. Engineers. A couple guys are professors at SDSU."

"How far away is Mexico?" Sybil asked.

"Only three miles," Shelly replied. "We get illegal aliens running through here from time to time, so be sure to always lock your house. There've been a couple burglaries."

Sybil's eyes went a little wide. "No kidding? They actually come into the neighborhood?"

Shelly nodded with pride. Mesa Vista's proximity to Mexico was a quirk that Shelly perceived as somehow giving the area distinction. "Now and then the Border Patrol helicopter flies over the neighborhood at night, and it sounds like there's a war on or something. Scared hell out of me when I first heard it."

"Well," Ruskin said, sipping his drink, "it's a good thing I decided not to sell my pistols." He reached into the front pocket of his knit shirt and withdrew what was obviously a marijuana cigarette. "Do you folks . . . imbibe?"

"You bet," I said heartily, but I was taken aback. I smoked it from time to time, but always with discretion. I had a security clearance to worry about, as did most of the guys I smoked with. Just popping out a joint in front of strangers did not strike me as terribly bright.

We passed the joint around. Ruskin told us a little about his job. He was an attorney working in the legal department of Techlydyne, a medium-big outfit that I knew had a few juicy contracts going. It made me wonder why he had bought a place in Mesa Vista, which is nice enough but definitely not in the high-powered lawyer-doctor league. "Been with Techlydyne since I got out of law school." He took another hit, held it, let it out. "Which hasn't been all that long ago. I went to law school rather late, due to a little stint in the Air Force."

"Oh?" I said, uninterested. That he had been in the service was no surprise. And without his saying so, I knew he had been an officer, too. He had the look of a man grown accustomed to giving orders.

The girls began talking to each other in a way that excluded Ruskin and me. Clubs, community affairs—what in unenlightened times had been called woman talk. I got up, picking up two empty glasses. "Excuse me while I make a fresh batch."

"I'll come with you." Ruskin picked up the other two glasses.

Now that I was standing, I could feel the effects of the grass. It had been weeks since I'd had some. I felt warm and marshmallowy, and when the girls giggled at something, it sounded like tinkling bells.

Ruskin put the glasses down and sat on a barstool on the dining area side of the counter. I dumped some ice in the blender and pressed the button, and the clattering was extremely loud. Ruskin grimaced at the noise but still managed to smile his friendly smile. He looked a little older than I, maybe thirty-six or so.

I went through the drink preparation slowly, the dope making me clumsy. I laughed at one of my goofs, as one will under the influence, and Ruskin's smile broadened so that I could see his pearly whites. I felt good. The Marshes looked as if they were going to be all-right neighbors.

"Your wife told me you were transferred from San Francisco."

"That's right." He took another hit from the almost-gone joint, then handed it to me. "Stupid shits lost twenty-four million dollars last year, so they're consolidating everything down here. Techlydyne will be totally gone from San Francisco in another year."

"That's an interesting bit of news," I lied.

"It's so different here. It's really weird, you know? Living out in the desert like this."

"Well, this isn't exactly the desert. That's on the other side of mountains. This is more like prairie."

He shrugged. "Whatever. It looks like you could film a cattle rustler movie out here." And that was true, but it was something I had so gotten used to I no longer noticed it.

"There're some coyotes still out here," I said. "A lady down the street had her dog killed by one, can you believe it?"

He shook his head in polite disbelief. I hurried with the drinks, anxious to get back to the living room and have another look at Ruskin's wife. He was an okay guy, but I didn't feel like kibitzing in the kitchen all night. I poured the icy green goo into the glasses.

Ruskin had gotten off his stool and was admiring an old print that hung in an unobtrusive corner of the dining area. "Interesting," he said over his shoulder. "Isn't this *Ophelia* . . . by Millais?"

I could have been no more startled than if he had told me he was from the planet Mars. I peered over the counter, squinting at the picture that, like the surrounding topography, I had gotten so used to I was no longer aware of it. I wasn't even sure where I had gotten it.

Then I remembered. College. I had bought it in college, and it was indeed *Ophelia*, painted by Sir John Everett Millais.

I came around the counter, drinks in hand, and gave Ruskin his. "That's right," I said uncertainly. "I . . . bought the print by mail and made the frame myself."

He nodded briefly. "Good job."

The picture jumped out at me as if I were looking at it for the first time. It was of Hamlet's girlfriend Ophelia, who, having finally gone crazy, was lying face up in a river. She was on the verge of death, but serene. It was painted with a lush realism, weirdly sumptuous in its beautiful detail. I suddenly remembered why I had liked it so, way back when. The beautiful painting with a macabre theme. I had once found it endlessly fascinating.

Ruskin sipped his drink. "I've always liked this school of paint-ers, the Pre-Raphaelites. I think they've been much underrated, don't you?"

I looked at Ruskin, then at the painting. "Yes. Very much so."

Ruskin sipped his drink. "I've often wondered why they called themselves that. The Pre-Raphaelites. Have any idea?"

Much to my surprise I did not have to rummage around for the correct memories, unexamined as they had been for so long. They bubbled up like a clear, sweet spring. The Pre-Raphaelite Brotherhood—Millais, who had been only twenty-three when he painted *Ophelia*. William Holman Hunt. Ford Madox Brown. Dante Gabriel Rossetti . . . God! Had I really known and loved their works so intimately? Had I really been like that?

I spoke softly, staring at the painting. "They called themselves Pre-Raphaelites because they so admired the bold colors used by the old Italian masters, back before the time of Raphael."

"You've studied art history, then."

"No, at least not formally. It was just something . . . I was once interested in."

He smiled and nodded, then put his hand on my shoulder. "Come on, Charles. Can't leave the ladies by themselves too long, can we?"

We went to the living room. A four-way conversation ensued,

something about the pros and cons of the various home comput-
ers. But my mind wasn't on the discussion. Nor was it on Mrs.
Marsh, whose generous bust moved with such fetching symme-
try as she excitedly explained the advantages of two disk drives.

Ruskin's offhand comment about *Ophelia* had jarred me more
than I had thought possible. I could not remember the last time
I had talked with someone about something so esoteric as a
painting. Mortgages, yes. Divorces, yes. Office politics and stock
market performance, yes, yes, yes.

But paintings?

Ah, but once I did have such conversations, and had them all
the time. I had sincerely cared about such things. And not only
paintings, but film, philosophy, ethics, architecture—those and a
thousand other things. It was a time when each day held promise
of wondrous excitement, when the world was opening up like a
sweetly exotic flower.

So different now.

I went back into the kitchen and worked on a fresh batch of
drinks. So I had liked talking about that sort of thing when I was
in college. So what? That was appropriate for an unfettered boy
in the fantasy world of college. Now things were different. Now I
was a full-grown man with a home and a wife and a career, and it
was inevitable that some things should slip by the wayside. That
was the way things worked. For everybody.

I pressed the blender's button and the machine clattered to
life. I looked at Ruskin in the living room, who was grinning and
nodding as Shelly talked. He looked every inch the adroit corporate climbateer, and yet I wondered. Wondered if there was
something more to him, if he had somehow managed to hold on
to a bit of what he had been like when his mind was beginning to
open, before the crush of maturity and responsibility had clipped
those wings. And, by extension, had also managed to make other
things work to his liking.

I wondered if that was the case. And what the secret was to
being like that.

It broke up around eleven. This time the Marshes exited by
way of the front door, and as we stood there telling each other

how pleased we were to have met, there came the far-off, bale-ful howl of a coyote. It was faint, but eerie nonetheless, like the soundtrack in a horror movie when they give you the first glimpse of Castle Dracula.

Maybe it was the grass, but something about it made me smile. Ruskin smiled too, looking at me as if he knew what was passing through my mind. His smile grew into a grin, and then he began chuckling. It was infectious. We all started laughing, and though there was a faint undertone of nervous self-consciousness, it was hearty enough.

Three

That Monday after I'd met the Marshes I couldn't get my mind on work. And since the guy who shared my office wasn't in—Ed Farley had been making it more of a ritual to be too hung over to show up Monday mornings—I didn't have to pretend to be busy. I merely propped my shoes on the desk, leaned back in the swivel chair, and stared out at the eighteenth-story view. Short, square buildings marched down to the waterfront. The single, graceful line of the Coronado Bridge curved across the sparkling bay. A green helicopter flew low over the bridge, chattering toward North Island Naval Air Station. From this angle Coronado appeared more woodsy than it actually was, its Mayberry R.F.D. skyline dominated by the red cone of the Hotel Del Coronado.

Nice view. Nice city. *My* city, even though ten years ago I wasn't sure exactly where it was. Then I had been just another slaphappy college joe, thoroughly enjoying myself at Chapel Hill. What brought me west was an ROTC obligation—duty aboard the U.S.S. *Groves*, a guided-missile destroyer. Her homeport was San Diego, but most of the time I was aboard we cruised the Gun Line off the coast of Vietnam, which was still very hot in those days. Shelly I had met and married in Los Angeles, while the *Groves* was in the Long Beach Naval Shipyard for a lengthy overhaul. She had been a grade-school teacher, a fresh graduate of UCLA.

My ROTC obligation was over before I was ready to get out of the Navy. The four years that had once seemed like an eternity had somehow managed to go by like a rocket. I took shore duty in San Diego, making sure I had a billet that put me in frequent contact with the local defense-related industries. When the time was right I resigned my commission and signed on with Aerotel. They had been impressed with my tour as missile officer aboard the *Groves*, with my job as overhaul manager in Long Beach, and, of course, with the way I could take a rough blueprint and muscle it all the way through production and wind up with something that worked in real life. My liberal arts degree was overlooked in the same manner as a pot bust or a drunk driving conviction—a forgivable youthful peccadillo.

Shelly and I did little soul-searching in deciding to settle in San Diego. A native of Los Angeles, Shelly found the slower pace of San Diego much to her liking. And there was nothing that made me want to go back to Raleigh. Even my Southern accent—not very strong to begin with, like most North Carolinians—had completely disappeared.

And the years went by with astonishing speed. I was firmly implanted on the treadmill of upward mobility. I went from line engineer to management. We bought the house in Mesa Vista. Our circle of friends grew, and Shelly and I were content in our role as Attractive Young Couple.

Then we lost the baby.

All I remember of that black time was that I kept telling myself it wasn't so, that this had not been in the game plan, that Attractive Young Couples were not touched by such things. Even when I dismantled the crib in the never-to-be-used nursery, I had the feeling I wasn't really there, that I was staggering through some horribly long nightmare and would wake up any day, any day.

But it was real, all right. As real and hard and irrefutable as a ten-ton boulder.

One black day slowly ground into the next, and the time finally came when whole days would go by without thinking of the lost baby. Then weeks.

It changed Shelly. Lines appeared on her face, bracketing her eyes and mouth. The blue in her eyes had gently faded. She was still glad enough to go to neighborhood parties, but she no longer let loose with that wild laugh whenever she heard a good joke. She had not gone back to teaching. Her biggest accomplishment had been to join the Family Fitness Center.

And me? A certain heaviness had settled on my face, giving a soft focus to my features. It was getting more difficult to keep off the excess poundage, but that did not seem so important anymore. And the job . . . for some reason I found myself paying close attention to the details of Aerotel's retirement policy—a matter that I had once found impossibly dull.

I watched the bright cars snaking across the Coronado Bridge, the sun making bright highlights against chrome and windshield. A frigate was coming up the channel from the 32nd Street Naval Station, sedate at the harbor's speed limit of twelve knots.

I suddenly recollected a late-night beer bust back in college; one of my buddies had pronounced that a decade hence none of us would be doing anything remotely connected to our boyish dreams.

How right he had been!

My eyes closed as I let my mind drift back to those days. Then I had been so hopped up with the pure pleasure of uncovering new ideas it seemed I was on a drug that increased the heartbeat a hundredfold. I could spend days without sleep, absorbing books like Big Macs, screwing all night with a pickup from a 16mm showing of an Ingmar Bergman film, and still manage to bluff my way through an early morning oral exam.

Or spend hours and hours talking with someone about the subtle beauty of a painting like *Ophelia*.

"Mr. Ripley?"

I dropped my feet to the floor and swiveled toward the door. "Yes, Vicki?"

"I finally got that material together, all ready to go." She smiled as she extended a single piece of paper. "All you have to do is sign the cover letter."

"Fine. Hand it over."

Vicki walked toward my desk, the missive proudly extended.

Vicki Kimberly was short but the proportions were perfectly correct, hair and eyes both brown. A modest slit in her skirt hinted at some very well-made legs. Vicki was one of the six girls from the secretarial pool who tended to Ed's or my correspondence needs. Vicki had lately made it a point to take care of all of mine.

I took the letter and scanned it briefly. It was to an acquaintance of mine, a lieutenant commander out at Miramar Naval Air Station. He had requested specs on a new airborne radar we were just testing. I caught two typos and handed it back.

"Cheez, I'm sorry about that, Mr. Ripley." Her lips were a

thoughtful pout. "I ran the text through the spelling checker before I got out the hard copy."

"That's all right, Vicki. It shouldn't take you two seconds to get it fixed." How someone could screw up a two-paragraph letter on a word processor was beyond me. But then she was only . . . nineteen? Twenty? Tanned. Boy, she must spend all her time at the beach.

She started to go but something made me want to talk to her more. "Doing anything for lunch?"

Puzzled. "No."

"Then how about joining me?"

Genuine pleasure. "Sure. That'd be great."

The anticipation of having lunch with Vicki changed my morning. Put a nice rosy glow on it. I happily wondered what we would talk about, if it would be the same sort of conversation I'd participated in when I was her age.

Her age . . .

And when Ed Farley staggered in bleary-eyed and moaning, I was acutely conscious of where I stood between these two people: a little more than a decade each way. On the one end bright eyes and clear skies, on the other shaking hands and despair. I was glad I was not going to lunch with Ed, or even with one of my contemporaries. I had no stomach for talk about the latest milspec change for the B-1's backup inertial nav system. Lunch with Vicki would be clear, fresh water, sweet and refreshing.

I took her to an actual restaurant instead of the delicatessen I usually frequented. It was a mom-and-pop Italian affair, a little cheap on the furnishings but truly gourmet food-wise. A fat, bald man took our orders as if he were doing us a great favor. Vicki took in the atmosphere avidly, her brown eyes bright and alive, posture erect and trim. Her two-piece business suit, severe except for the slit skirt, actually made her look younger than she probably was, as if she were in the attic trying on Mom's old clothes.

"Do you eat here much, Mr. Ripley?"

"Charles."

She smiled. "Charles. God, I can't believe you asked me to lunch."

I shrugged and grinned. "What's so strange about that?"

"Well, I've been at that office practically a whole year and you didn't seem to notice me at all."

Her knee brushed against mine accidentally-on-purpose and her smile broadened. The fat waiter came back and set down the carafe of wine I'd ordered, sighed as he plunked down two five-and-dime wineglasses. I poured and Vicki raised her glass in toast. We clinked rims and I forced a jovial grin. "So you've been with Aerotel a year. Where were you before that?"

She frowned in concentration. Remington, Indiana, turned out to be where she was born and bred. Shortly after high school graduation she and a girlfriend had come to see what California was all about. The girlfriend went back home after a year but Vicki stayed, working in a clothing store in Mission Beach and taking classes at City College.

"But it's so hard working and going to school at the same time, you know? I dropped out when I saw an ad for secretaries here. Besides, I got what I wanted out of that place, which was how to work those word processors."

"You didn't finish the business course?"

"They don't really check on that at Aerotel, didn't you know? Besides, they got their own secretarial training program anyway."

"Didn't like college?"

She lifted her shoulders. "It was okay. I mean, you can take it or leave it. You went to college, didn't you?"

"Uh-huh."

"And it was a real college, wasn't it? Not like a two-year college."

"Yeah, it was a real college."

She nodded and smiled. "Then you were a Navy officer, weren't you?"

"How did you know that?"

Again, that brush on the knee. "You're so different than the other guys I know. I mean, besides from being so much older."

"Huh?"

She leaned on the table and looked at me earnestly. "Most guys

I know act like they're working on a jigsaw puzzle and don't even know where to start. I mean, they try to act cool and everything but they really don't know what the hell's going on."

"I see," I said judiciously.

She sipped her wine and looked at me speculatively. "I like a guy who really has his shit together."

I looked at her and spread my hands in a helpless gesture. This conversation wasn't anything like what I thought it would be. But if she could be blunt, so could I. "Read any good books lately?"

She considered the question seriously, her eyes rolling up and to the left as she opened mental filing cabinets. "I'm right in the middle of *Savage Surrender,* and it's pretty good." She looked at me directly. "How about you?"

"No. I haven't read anything good in quite some time."

We talked of music, or rather I listened to Vicki catalog a list of strange-sounding groups. The fettucine arrived, and according to my taste buds' report it was delicious. But I didn't enjoy it. How could I, feeling like such an idiot?

I had wanted to commune with that thrill of learning and growing that I had known in college. Which was impossible, of course. I could no more recapture that pleasure than I could regain my actual bodily youth. Looking at Vicki made me feel not only stupid, but more lonesome than ever. And blackest of all, I began to toy with the suspicion that the best part of my life might have already passed me by.

But why did it have to be that way? Look at someone like that Ruskin Marsh fellow. *He* seemed well-satisfied with who and what he was. A complex man who might even *thrive* on his own complexity ... rather than letting it torment. Maybe there was hope. Maybe there was a way.

I tried looking at the situation from different angles.

Okay, I thought. All right. So I wasn't a boy anymore. I was a grown man, and knew something of the world and how it worked. And was this not better? So I could have once sat up all night discussing the fine points of, say, American foreign policy over a pitcher of beer. Well, not too long ago I had been off the coast of Vietnam, witness to the spectacle of helicopters fleeing the U.S. Embassy, surely the greatest failure of foreign policy in this country's history. How did that compare with a bunch of inexperienced boys debating how many angels could dance on the head of a pin?

Of course, while it was happening—and not only that but when two MiGs made a strafing run on the *Groves* and watching a sailor getting his arm chewed off in a winch and the nights with the bar girls in Olongapo and a thousand other things—I had done nothing but let the event wash over me unexamined. The evacuation from Saigon had just been another busy op. My mind had been off.

I could see now that that had been a mistake. To live an unexamined life was to live in only one dimension. My work, my home, my wife—those things had become so familiar they no longer satisfied.

Henceforward things would be different. I would open my eyes, as, perhaps, Ruskin Marsh had opened his. Maybe that was his secret.

And was not my present life far more richly textured than that of a college boy?

So lunch finished on an upbeat note. I was eager to conclude the day and get home. I wanted to drop by the Marshes, perhaps under the pretext of borrowing something. Maybe Ruskin might invite me into his den, if den he had, and we might talk . . .

I smiled. It had been a long time since I had been interested in knowing what made a particular person tick, male or female. Yet I wanted to talk with Ruskin. And, when you got down to it, be his friend.

And when was the last time I had wanted to be friends with someone? Perhaps this was a good sign. The new me in action.

I paid the check, and when Vicki snaked her arm through mine I hardly noticed the pressure of a firm young breast against my bicep.

Four

But the rest of the day was given over to a late-hours flap, and by the time I staggered home at nine the only thing I wanted to take on was "Monday Night Baseball" and white wine. The following days were similarly occupied. Much as I wanted, I couldn't get around to visiting Ruskin. About all I could do was wave hello when I saw him getting into his Porsche 944 each morning. It was a bright, glossy copper color, and if he had many more toys like that I could see why he couldn't afford a slightly better development than Mesa Vista.

Sybil and Shelly saw a lot of each other. Monday they had driven down to the Family Fitness Center in Chula Vista for a workout, and this was repeated on Wednesday and then again on Friday. Shelly would return from these sessions flushed and healthy, and when she cooked dinner she hummed so loud I could hear her in the living room.

It was nice they had hit it off so well. Shelly hadn't made any really close friends in the neighborhood, and the effects of her new friendship were pleasantly obvious. And, of course, it wasn't hard on the eyes when I caught the occasional glimpse of Sybil walking away from our garage and waving good-bye, her electric-blue bodysuit clinging and stained with perspiration.

I looked forward to the weekend, when there would time to drop by and give Ruskin a visit.

But as I ate breakfast Saturday, I looked at the nearby picture of *Ophelia* and had second thoughts. How exactly would I go about it? Rap at the door and say Ruskin, old boy, how about knocking off mowing the lawn so we can talk about Art and Beauty? I thought of the fervor I had felt during the lunch with Vicki Kimberly, of the feeling that being Ruskin's friend would somehow help to change my life. My cheeks grew warm.

So when Shelly suggested we go on a shopping expedition, I immediately assented. We drove into Chula Vista in Shelly's used

Valiant station wagon. It turned out to be a very busy and not
unpleasant day. We had lunch at a place that was thicketed with
baskets of leafy ferns. Shelly bought several more exercise outfits.
I picked up a nice Ralph Lauren blazer on sale at Robinson's.

Dinner was hamburgers on the outdoor grill, made tastier by
the little stub of marijuana cigarette Ruskin had left in our ash-
tray last week. We watched television for a while but there was
nothing on, so Shelly and I decided on a late-night session in the
Jacuzzi . . . and one thing led to another and I got out and turned
off the exterior lights and shucked my trunks and Shelly and I
made love in the darkness, surrounded by the frizzing seltzer
sound of the Jacuzzi. And I told myself that thoughts of Ruskin
were far away, that if a friendship occurred, it should come natu-
rally and easily, and not be rushed.

Sunday I awoke totally refreshed and full of ambition. I started
organizing my few shop tools in the garage, cordoning off a work
area. Soon it got hot and I pressed the button on the garage door
opener (put it in myself, a two-day job) and the slab of wood
swiveled up and out of the way. Some cooler air came in, but it
offered little refreshment. I stripped off my shirt and continued
work in my faded cutoffs.

Shelly brought out a giant roast beef sandwich and a cold beer
around noon. It was delicious. She was decked out in her striped
gym outfit, and told me she was going to spend the rest of the
afternoon with Sybil at the fitness center. I nodded as I worked on
the thick sandwich.

By the time I had everything arranged, I had already outlined
my first project. A bookcase, custom-made to accommodate the
paperbacks that were now overflowing the cardboard boxes in
the spare bedroom. I began examining the pieces of scrap wood
in the corner, figuring dimensions, wondering how much more I
would have to buy. Perhaps I really would turn that spare room
into a study.

"Hello, Charles."

I turned around, startled. It was Ruskin, standing just outside
the garage, bathed in sunlight.

"How you doing, buddy?" I got off my haunches and smiled
with pleasure.

"Been working out back," he said as he stepped in. He wore shorts and a sweat-stained T-shirt, big black sunglasses. "I was wondering if I could borrow your lawn trimmer."

"Sure." I waved to where the Black & Decker hung from a stud. "Help yourself."

He took it off the wall. "Great. I'll have it back this afternoon."

"Don't worry."

He handled the trimmer as if it were something finely made. It seemed as if he had something on his mind but did not know how to go about saying it. "Is this your workshop?"

I nodded as I wiped sweat from my forehead. He stepped near the workbench and gave a friendly little smile. "Nice arrangement."

"I'm getting ready to make a bookcase. Going to turn the spare bedroom into a study."

"Really? I finally got mine all set up." He grinned. "First thing I do whenever we move."

I was trying to figure out why he was acting bashful. Could it be that he wanted to be friends as badly as I? And was as equally shy? "I'd like to see your study sometime. Get some ideas."

"Well . . ." he looked down at the trimmer, smiling. "Come on over and take a look now. We'll pop a couple beers."

Something inside glowed warmly. "Sure. Let me get a shirt."

I went through the garage's back door, across the open walkway, then into the laundry room. One of my big Hawaiian shirts hung from the rod, and I buttoned it on.

Ruskin and I walked to his house, and I noticed it was starting to get a little overcast, which was strange for this time of year. The front door was unlocked and we went inside. There was a hat rack in the hallway, and a few framed prints. It looked like the interior of any other house in Mesa Vista. We went into his study.

The first thing that caught my eye was the bookcase, which was by far the largest I'd ever seen in the home of a personal acquaintance. Not that it was gigantic—it was only the width of two refrigerators—but I was totally unaccustomed to seeing anything more than a couple of shelves in anyone's home. The bookcase itself was oak, old, well-made; an anomaly against the bland white walls and meager proportions of the room. A big

rolltop desk dominated another wall. Hanging above his desk
were three hunting rifles, stocks smooth and glossy, the black
machined works glistening with oil. Two squat filing cabinets
were next to the desk, and on top of them was one of those small,
boxlike refrigerators.

Ruskin sat in the executive-style swivel chair and opened the
icebox. He gave me a Coors Light and I worked the tab and took
a quick gulp. It was so cold I felt little slivers of ice going down
my throat. I sat in the only other chair in the small room, a Barcalounger apparently made of genuine leather.

Ruskin opened a desk drawer and withdrew a marijuana cigarette. "Like to get a little high?"

"Okay."

He lit it, puffed, handed it over. "Careful. This is legendary
stuff. One toke will do it."

I took a hit, and still holding it in, nodded toward the guns.
"Hunt?"

"Used to quite a bit. Now it's just"—a small shrug—"a hobby.
These days I'm more of a gun collector than a hunter. Haven't
hunted for years, actually."

I let out the smoke. "Your entire collection?"

"No, I've got a forty-five in the bedroom. And this." He slid
open a side drawer, withdrew a small automatic, black and gleaming. "A Beretta. A three-eighty." He put it back, then reached
down and slid open the desk's file drawer. "And this little number
here, which is my pride and joy. One of these days I'm going to
have a special mount made for it." He held up a small machine
gun, a weapon that looked like something a commando might
use. It was so small it was rather like a large pistol. A long magazine extended from the bottom of the pistol grip.

He handed it over with a proud smile. I was surprised at its
light weight.

"It's an Ingram," Ruskin explained. "A Model Ten, nine mil-
limeter. Unique weapon. See the silencer?"

How could I miss it? Sticking out of the main works was a
thick silencer tube, longer even than the Ingram's frame.

"It actually makes it fire more accurately," Ruskin said. "The
exact opposite of what silencers do for other weapons."

I felt a little stoned already. I handed the Ingram back. "But that's a commercial model, right? It's just semi-automatic, isn't it?"

Ruskin smiled down at the weapon, handling it fondly. "It was. But that was pretty simple to fix." He leveled the gun at the bookcase, and began swinging the barrel in wide, lazy arcs.

"You ought to try firing it on full auto," he said. "It's . . . astonishing, really. And kind of gratifying." Then, with a sigh, he put the gun back in the file door and slid it closed.

I puffed lightly on the cigarette. Next to the bookcase were the various memorabilia of his career. A black-and-white photo of a much younger Ruskin, standing behind a dead deer and holding on to one of those elaborate bows that have pulleys and cables connecting the upper and lower limbs. A framed degree from Hastings Law School, proclaiming to all who should see these presents that Ruskin Albert Marsh was a Juris Doctor. His last Air Force commission, which was for the rank of major. A little wooden plaque from the unit in which he had evidently served, the 666th Tactical Fighter Wing, the insignia for which was a screaming eagle, the logo underneath reading *The Howling Bastards*.

I became aware I'd been holding on to the joint for some time. I was truly stoned. I handed it back. "You've got some library," I said.

"Joined Book of the Month a long time ago. I still haven't read some of them. Matter of fact, I'm still trying to get through the fucking Harvard Classics, and I'm only up to *Moby Dick*." He gingerly snubbed out the cigarette. "I've always loved to read."

"So have I."

"Well, then." Ruskin got out of his chair and went to the bookcase. "You'd probably like to take a look at this." He took out an old, leather-bound book and handed it over. "Consider this ransom for your lawn trimmer."

The book was beautifully made, but it wasn't as old as I had thought. Looked brand new, in fact. There was no lettering on the cover or spine, just ornate scrollwork that seemed vaguely Islamic. I opened it and after three blank, creamy pages there was *Juliette or the Fortunes of Vice* and the author's name, the one and only Marquis de Sade. "I've heard of this," I said. "How is it?"

"It's kind of old-timey, but it's still fairly interesting." Ruskin sat back in his chair. "I'd like to hear your impressions after you've read it."

We talked of other books, and though the dope made the conversation a little nonsensical, it was still very pleasant. Almost like my college days, I suddenly realized, and felt a small rush of pleasure. I talked about some mysteries I especially liked, and Ruskin had read the more famous ones. I finished my beer and Ruskin handed me another. The air conditioning hissed gently from a vent near the ceiling. It was very nice.

The phone buzzed. It was one of those cordless remotes, and Ruskin picked up the slender handset. It had a small antenna. "Yes? Oh, hello, Sybil . . ."

I looked over *Juliette* while he talked. The leather was supple, almost oily to the touch. A very finely made thing. I wondered how he had come by it.

Ruskin recradled the phone in its charger housing. "That was the ladies. Seems they met up with someone Sybil knew, and they're going to be a little late coming home."

"How late?"

"Sounded like they might go somewhere for drinks. Sybil told me to go ahead and make my own dinner." He shook his head and smiled, as if indicating he had no talent in this area. "Charles, how about you and I going somewhere and getting ourselves something decent? I could use a big, thick steak, couldn't you?"

This sounded exactly like what I wanted to do. "Sure. That'd be great. But what about your son?"

"He's supposed to be eating with the Hapscombs tonight. I think he's probably already over there."

"Well, then. I'll just go get cleaned up."

"Fine. Let me shower and I'll meet you in my driveway in a few minutes."

Five

I went home and threw *Juliette* on top of a cardboard box full of paperbacks, then had a quick shower. I took some care in selecting clothes, dressing in what passed for strict formality out here—a jacket but no tie. It was a strange sensation, getting ready for an evening without Shelly. Reminded me of what it was like in the service, when I used to go out on the town with a few guys from the ship, searching for booze and good food, and maybe a few nightclubs where there might be some action. I brushed my hair, grinning at the mirror.

I left a note for Shelly, telling her I had gone out with Ruskin. I went around the house and turned on a few lights and locked the doors, then went over to Ruskin's driveway. He was coming out his front door, straightening the collar on his blue blazer. It was late afternoon, and the sky was completely overcast. There was the barest hint of moisture against my face, a mist that was almost rain. It would be good to have some rain; this was the season for brush fires.

We got in the copper Porsche. Ruskin twisted the key and the engine thrummed to life, then settled into a low, throaty purr. The interior smelled of well-cared-for leather.

"Nice car," I said.

"She's my one and only honey." He grunted as he released the handbrake, then began backing out. "Always wanted one of these babes. Got it on a special deal from a friend of mine up in San Francisco."

He drove through Mesa Vista a little fast, making his turns and shifting gears in a very efficient, businesslike sort of way. Once we were on the main road he punched in the cigarette lighter. After a moment, he took it out and lit . . . yet another marijuana cigarette, I saw. We took turns handing it back and forth. Ruskin tossed the tiny unsmoked part out the window. I settled back, feeling warm and content. Music quietly flowed from an all-encompassing

speaker system. It was that contemporary, progressive sort of
jazz, with separate instruments working frantically at different
tempos, rushing to nowhere. Maybe it was the dope, but I liked it.
I liked it a lot. I turned and looked at Ruskin. He had both hands
on the wheel, smiling as he engaged in the small pleasure of driving his expensive car.

Yes, indeed. This reminded me very much of my footloose
days. The evening stretched before me, now full of all kinds of
promise.

I felt like talking. "How did you like the Air Force?"

He shrugged indifferently. "I hated it. But Vietnam was okay."

"Really? Where were you stationed?"

"Thailand. Flew missions right out of Ubon, usually over
Hanoi and Haiphong."

"Were you in B-52s?"

"Nope. I drove an F-105. An F-105D Thunderchief."

"Ah. Fighter jock, eh?"

"Yep." Mist began to dot the windshield. Ruskin flicked on the
wipers. It was the pulse mode: one swash of the wipers, three
seconds, another swash. "Seems like a billion years ago now."
He turned on the headlights, giving a little sigh of fond remem-
brance. "Seems like I was on another planet."

"See much action?"

The wipers swept across the windshield. Stopped. "Got a MiG
once."

"No kidding. Tell me about it."

His grin broadened. The wipers did another single sweep. "We
were over Haiphong on a photo recon mission, going along at
thirty thousand feet. I was just escort; there wasn't any photo
gear on my ship, except for the gun cameras. We were expecting
SAMs, but that day the Cong tried something different. They sent
some of their new MiG-21s up for an intercept." Ruskin shook his
head and smiled. His hands tightened on the wheel. "So everybody split up chop-chop. I rolled to the right and dove, cutting in
the burner to go supersonic. That hurried things up." He shifted
a little on the leather seat, hiking himself forward. "There was a
MiG ten thousand feet below, coming almost straight up. He had
already fired one of his Atolls, and was pouring on the cannon

fire. His nose was lit up like a goddamn Christmas tree. The Atoll was no sweat—it was a heat-seeker, and totally wasted on a nose-to-nose shot. I broke right and went down under him, then pulled up sharp, real sharp, as sharp as I could make that Thud pull. It was a tight maneuver, and I immediately went subsonic." His hands worked harder at the steering wheel. "He was rolling over, trying to come back down, but I had my pipper right on his tailpipe. I got a positive growl over my headset—this noise the Sidewinder transmits when it senses a heat source it can home in on—and pulled the trigger. The bird dropped from my wing and went straight at him. The MiG started evasive maneuvers." Ruskin grinned, staring fixedly at the road. "Just before I came to his level, that bird came home to roost. Right up his fucking ass. I gained a little altitude and rolled over."

I was totally absorbed. It no longer seemed Ruskin was in the world of flat dimensions, but up in the sky where there were three, jammed into the cramped cockpit of an F-105. "So when the nose finally got pointing back at the ground I can see the gook's chute. The cocksucker's bailed out. I continued diving." He gave a strange little laugh. "So the chute's all of a sudden lined up in my gunsight display, just as pretty as you please. I pressed my thumb against the twenty-millimeter cannon button and"— Indeed, I could see his thumb squeezing tight on the wheel— "and man, you could feel the whole plane shaking. That Vulcan was made to put out six thousand rounds per minute, and believe me, that guy came apart like he was made of wet paper. Then I pulled up."

He slowly relaxed, settling back in the seat. The mist was coming down a little harder now. Ruskin flicked the windshield lever and the blades began sweeping continuously. I reran the story in my stoned mind. "So you ... shot the guy in his parachute?"

There was surprise in his voice. "Sure."

"But isn't that against the Geneva Convention, or something?"

He looked at me incredulously. "He was a *gook!*" He shook his head, hands retightening on the wheel. "Geneva Convention," he said disgustedly. "You know what the Cong did with captured pilots? You ever see those parades in Hanoi with a couple of jocks as Grand Marshall?" He snorted. "I was glad to blow that guy out of the sky, and I didn't care if he was in a MiG or riding a fucking broom."

I didn't say anything. The wipers beat steadily.

"Ah, but I really enjoyed flying, Charles." There was no longer any anger in his voice. He was back to the fond-remembrance mode. "I used to take my ship way the hell up. Sometimes I went so high the atmosphere actually began to darken. Drove the guys on the ground crazy when I did that. They'd start yelling over the radio for me to come back down to my assigned altitude. But I'd just keep on going until the controls wouldn't respond anymore." He chuckled.

We pulled into the parking lot of a new-looking restaurant on the edge of Chula Vista. The lot was almost full even though it was still fairly early. We found a slot, and walked quickly through the drizzle to the front door.

There was no table just yet; perhaps a half-hour's wait, according to an apologetic maitre d'. Ruskin and I went to the jammed bar. Scotch and water for us both. I reached for my wallet.

"I'll take this round," Ruskin said. He laid down a ten and told the bartender to keep the change.

Five minutes later we found ourselves at a good table, huge menus offered up by the maitre d' himself.

It looked expensive, but what the hell. I was famished. I ordered twelve bucks' worth of two-inch-thick roast beef. Ruskin went for their top-of-the-line item, which was the steak-and-lobster special. We ordered more drinks, which confused the young waitress.

"The cocktail waitress is supposed to take care of that," she explained.

Ruskin put down the menu and looked at her patiently. "I'd like to see the manager, please."

She looked startled. "Manager? But—"

A little steel crept into his voice. "Will you kindly get the manager, girl?"

She nodded and left. Ruskin shook his head in exasperation. "Stupid cunt," he murmured.

The manager arrived and Ruskin gave a little lecture on the

nature of good service. The manager bobbed his head, quietly whispering apologies. The upshot was that we wound up with a new waitress, one that didn't give any backchat when it came to ordering more drinks.

Then we began talking. Ruskin had taken an afternoon off to visit the San Diego Museum of Art, and he thought it was pretty good "for a city this size." I didn't tell him San Diego actually had a bigger population than San Francisco.

It had been a long time since I'd visited the museum, but Ruskin's account brought it all back. We had a wonderful conversation, stimulating and occasionally funny. He had a surprisingly detailed knowledge of contemporary art. He told me his favorite artist was Claes Oldenburg, with Roy Lichtenstein a close second. We ordered more drinks.

Dinner came. Ruskin ordered a bottle of red wine, and when it came he poured me a glass without my asking. "Should go well with your beef," he said.

The food was delicious, and we continued our talk while we ate. The meat was richly satisfying, and the liquor seemed to elevate me a few inches from the booth. This was more the sort of meal I'd had in mind when I'd taken Vicki Kimberly out.

I watched Ruskin working at his steak, elbow pistoning as he cut into the thick meat. He was excellent company, as perceptive and witty as anyone I'd ever met. And yet there was something more, wasn't there? I thought of the man who'd brought an F-105's gunsights to bear upon the helpless form dangling at the bottom of a parachute. Tried to square it with the person who sat with me now. Couldn't, quite . . .

But then, why should it? So Ruskin didn't fit in a convenient pigeonhole. Shouldn't that work to arouse curiosity all the more?

Dinner finished and we topped things off with Irish coffees. My belly was full, and I felt pleasantly high. Ruskin waved toward the dance floor. "What say we mosey over there and see what's up? It's still early."

I looked at my watch. The time was a little difficult to make out at first, but eventually I reckoned it was quarter to nine. "Maybe I should call Shelly first, let her know—"

"Aw, what for? She knows you're out with me. And what are you going to tell her? That you want to stay out a little longer to scout out some stray pussy?"

We both chuckled. The check arrived and Ruskin immediately took it. "My pleasure." He took out an American Express Gold Card. "I can put this on my expense account."

I grinned lopsidedly. "Consultation with a client?"

He smiled. "And my counsel is to get ourselves over to the dance floor and see what's shakin'."

Why not? Shelly wouldn't have a heart attack if I stayed out a little late. Ruskin got up and I sidled out of the booth. Things spun a little as I got to my feet.

We moved to the dance area. All the cocktail tables were taken and it was standing room only. Music with a heavily repetitive beat flowed from an excellent speaker system. Very much like the discos I used to visit. My grin spread from ear to ear.

We made our way to the bar. It was so crowded Ruskin had to shoulder some people aside. A guy who spilled his drink seemed to blame it on Ruskin.

"Hey, watch where you're going, Jack." He was on the tall side, and had a huge, bushy mustache.

Ruskin edged nearer. "Yeah? You got a problem, bud?"

I stood beside Ruskin, trying to look mean. The tall guy looked us both over and turned away.

We made it to the bar and ordered fresh drinks. Ruskin surveyed the crowd with vast satisfaction. There were quite a few unattached young women.

"Say," I said. "I think that one on the other side's interested."

"Yeah? Where?"

I pointed her out. Two girls at a cocktail table, alone. One, a blonde with an elaborate hairdo, was playing with a straw and looking at Ruskin in an obvious way. Ruskin waved. The blonde smiled and turned to her friend, who had long, black hair. The two conferred, giggling.

Ruskin fortified himself with another stiff pull at his drink. "All right, Charles." He wiped his mouth with the back of his hand. "Into the breech, old boy."

We went over and introduced ourselves. We found two extra

chairs, and so made four places at the tiny cocktail table. Ruskin sat by the blonde. I took the brunette. They looked a lot older than they had from across the bar. Late thirties instead of late twenties. But any port in a storm, right?

The brunette's name was Mandy. Her face was just this side of being haggard, but her figure was ripely endowed. The other one, Hariette, looked as if she belonged in a trucker's honkytonk.

Ruskin entertained the ladies with some dirty jokes, and the punchlines never failed to make Hariette convulse with harsh brays. We ordered more drinks.

Mandy and I went to the dance floor. Things spun unpleasantly but the exercise began to sober me up. A slow number came and the woman pressed against me, rubbing her belly against my crotch suggestively. She looked up and said something very quietly. Vodka wisped from her mouth, but no intelligible words. I held her tighter, feeling the rough texture of her brassiere against my chest. She was a coarse, unattractive woman, but . . . I wanted her. I wanted to go someplace private and plow myself into her rich, tawdry body. I could see myself doing it. I could see it so clearly. Maybe I would even keep my socks on while I did it. I laughed, and Mandy looked a little puzzled at first, but she joined in, pressing against me tighter.

Now and then we went back to the table for a drink break. Mandy told me about herself. She was a divorcée, and had gotten a royal screwing of a settlement. Had to work as a cocktail waitress downtown. Most sonsabitches tipped like they were buying newspapers instead of drinks.

Ruskin and Hariette came back to the table, Hariette clinging to Ruskin and laughing. We ordered more drinks. Ruskin told some more dirty jokes, and both women held on to their sides as they shrieked. Now and then Ruskin would look at me and shake his head, as if saying *can you believe these two idiots?* Then he would tell Hariette another joke, caressing her leg as he whispered in her ear. The drinks went quickly.

Finally the girls went off to the powder room. Ruskin leaned over the table, his breath rich with the smell of bourbon. "We're going to a party, Charles."

"Huh?"

"That Hariette gal has invited us to a little party. She and Mandy are roommates."

"What kind of party?"

"Just the four of us." He winked.

I took another pull at my drink. "Just so long as we get home at a decent hour."

He shrugged. "Sure. We'll just get a couple blow jobs and be off. Back home in plenty of time."

The room spun lazily. "All right. Sure."

He slapped me on the shoulder. "Good man!" He chuckled as he buttoned up his blue blazer.

The girls came back and we went out into the parking lot. It was still drizzling, but no one seemed to mind getting wet. The air was slightly chilly, and it made me realize how drunk I was. We talked with the girls, and I saw from the way they were wobbling that they'd probably reached their limit, too. The arrangement was that they would drive in their car and we would follow. They got in a battered Pinto with plates that were two months expired.

At first I thought Ruskin might have had too much to drink, but he drove easily and well.

I started laughing to myself.

"What's so funny?"

"Oh, I . . . I just can't believe I'm doing this, Ruskin. It's been a long time since I've had an evening like this."

"Nothing like a knobber to round out the evening, eh? That used to be my favorite thing when I was in the service. Went to Bangkok every chance I got." He looked at me briefly. His face was softly lit by the green glow of the instrument lights. "Know what a blow job cost back then? A *nickel!*"

We laughed.

The northbound entrance for the freeway came up, but the little Pinto went on by.

"Now what the hell?" Ruskin gripped the wheel tighter. "I thought that was the on-ramp they were talking about."

"I—I don't remember if that was supposed to be the one or not."

"Is there another freeway further along this road?"

"I don't know. I don't think so."

We continued following the Pinto, going into a part of the county I did not know at all. It began to rain harder. My stomach twisted a little bit, and there was a faint wave of nausea. I leaned my head against the coolness of the window.

I was on the verge of dozing off when Ruskin began cursing.

"Goddamnit. Where the hell are we? Those cunts said they didn't live far away."

I looked around. All I could make out was that we were in a hilly area, driving up a long, curving road. Now and then I could see the lights of an infrequent house. I had no earthly idea where we were. I told Ruskin as much.

"Great!" he muttered.

We drove in silence for a few moments. Ruskin twisted restlessly. "Jesus," he said, "you know how long we've been following them? Half a goddamn hour! They must live in fucking L.A.!"

We continued up the hill. Then down the other side. Then up another hill.

"I can't take this anymore," Ruskin said, pressing on the accelerator. "These bitches are going to have to cut bait or fish."

He pulled up to their bumper and began honking the horn. He flicked his brights on and off. The Pinto slowed and pulled off to the side. Ruskin parked right behind. He got out, leaving the engine on, and I followed. It was not raining as heavily as it had looked from inside the car, but I pulled up my collar and jammed my hands into my pockets.

Ruskin walked to the driver's side of the Pinto and leaned in. He talked for a few moments, then I heard him shout, "*Lost?* What do you mean, *lost?*"

I sighed inwardly. How the hell had I gotten myself into this situation? I no longer wanted to screw some old hosebag. I wanted to go home and go to bed. I looked around. We were on a big hill. No houses nearby, but in the valley below and on another hill a mile or so away I could see the widely spaced lights of homes. Christ, if we went much farther, we'd wind up in the goddamn desert.

Ruskin finished talking with a "Just make it fast, then. We

haven't got all night." He walked back toward the Porsche and I got in.

"They said the on-ramp they usually use is out of service for repairs." He shook his head in exasperation. He slipped the gearshift into first. "Idiots."

The Pinto bit gravel as it took off from the shoulder. Ruskin shot onto the road, lips drawn in a tight line. The rear of the Porsche slipped a little, then the tires found their purchase.

"Stupid fucking bimbos," he muttered. "Too goddamn drunk to know where they are."

He was hunched forward, peering through the windshield. He looked down at the speedometer and grimaced. "Look at this! Forty miles an hour! *Jesus!*"

The Porsche's engine hummed louder as Ruskin applied speed, and we gained on the Pinto rapidly. He pulled up close, flicking his brights. *"C'mon,"* he yelled, as if the women could hear. *"Let's get this show on the road!"* He leaned on the horn.

The Pinto suddenly accelerated, pulling away. Ruskin let them gain distance, then brought up his speed to pace theirs. "All right." Ruskin's voice was back to normal. "Sixty. This is more like it."

We continued up the hill. The wipers beat steadily. Ruskin's arms swiveled to the right and left as he negotiated the turns. I watched the Pinto's taillights disappear as it crested a ridge. A moment later we roared over the rise.

Here the road dipped down. The Pinto was a hundred yards ahead, taillights enveloped in spray, barreling toward a sharp turn . . . and much, much too fast, I thought. I saw the brakelights flash bright red. The front of the Pinto began to turn, but the chunky rear end began to slew around. My heart leapt into my throat.

"Uh-oh," Ruskin whispered. He took his foot off the accelerator and the Porsche lost speed. "They're gonna lose it, Charles." He touched the brakes lightly, carefully slowing the car. "They're gonna lose it."

Though the Pinto was almost sideways it continued to scoot along, skidding toward the turn. The rear wheels were locked. No way they would make it, I suddenly realized. No way at all.

The Pinto trundled off the road and wobbled into the guardrail. A white-painted beam snapped out of the way, cartwheeling into the night. The Pinto abruptly dropped from view.

"Shit," Ruskin hissed. "Shit Christ almighty."

He brought the Porsche to a smooth but fast stop. We got out and ran to where the compact had splintered the old wooden guardrail. My heart was beating like a trip-hammer. We ran past the guardrail and looked down into a valley.

The Pinto was still going, rumbling down a steep hill, making a tremendous racket. It bucked and wobbled, then began rolling over sideways. It sounded like a hundred trash cans bouncing down an alley. I saw something fly off and sail into the night; a hubcap, I think.

"Great God," Ruskin said. "Great Christ."

The Pinto whanged into some kind of ditch, coming to a sudden halt. There were a few houses at the bottom of this valley, but the Pinto had landed in an undeveloped area. All we could hear was the whisper of the drizzling rain. The Pinto was about half a mile away.

And, very faintly, I made out the barest hint of a flame . . .

"Oh, shit," I said. "We've got to get to a phone, and fast."

I started to move but Ruskin grabbed my arm. "Wait a minute, Charles."

"What?"

"Are you planning to call the police?"

"Well, yes. Of course. The flame on the Pinto was brighter, licking skyward. "Call the police and the paramedics and—"

"And then what, Charles? We both reek of liquor. The police would have me on a breathalyzer in no time."

"But . . . but maybe I could say—"

"That *you* were driving?" Ruskin was very close, his face grimly intent. "Hell, *you've* had more to drink than *I*!"

There was a sudden, gentle *whump*. We looked at the Pinto. The fire was burning brighter now. Much brighter.

"There's nothing we can do for them," Ruskin said. "They're dead. What good would it do to call the police? Look, there're plenty of houses down there. Let one of them call it in."

I looked down in the valley. The Pinto was entirely engulfed in flames, going up like a dry haystack.

"Come on," he said. "There's nothing to connect us with this accident. All we have to do is simply leave and we're home free."

But I couldn't move. My feet were bolted to the ground, my eyes riveted to the burning Pinto. My heart fluttered as if it were a frightened bird.

"Come on, Charles!" Ruskin pulled at my arm. "We have everything to lose and nothing to gain!"

I saw the driver's door begin to open.

Ruskin stopped pulling at my sleeve.

The door finally swung free. A figure climbed out, arms flailing wildly. It was like a stick figure, with the sticks made of charcoal and everything else in flames. The figure staggered from the Pinto, arm-sticks clawing helplessly. It plowed around in a crazy circle, flames bright in the damp night. The stick figure stumbled and fell. It did not get back up. The flames rose high.

Ruskin licked his lips. "There. You see? There's nothing we can do for them. Let's get out of here."

We drove in silence. Ruskin continually flicked the radio from one station to another, dissatisfied with everything. I hunched down into the seat, thinking things over. We finally lucked onto a freeway on-ramp, then I knew where we were. Ruskin was immensely relieved.

He produced another marijuana cigarette and punched in the lighter. I declined his offer of a smoke. But after a few minutes I went ahead and had a few hits anyway. I saw a few landmarks that indicated Mesa Vista was only minutes away and told Ruskin which exit to look for.

I could see his grin in the glow of the instrument lights. "Home free, boy. Home free."

"Yeah. No sweat."

He took a hand off the wheel and gave me a little reassuring squeeze on the shoulder.

Six

Monday. The office seemed the same, right down to Ed not being at his desk. But then, why shouldn't it?

I sat at my desk and took another look at the morning paper. The story about the burned-out Pinto was on page two of the B section, and there was absolutely no hint that it was being treated as anything other than a routine accident. The coroner even noted there was an excessive amount of alcohol in the victims' blood.

Home free, Ruskin had said. Indeed, when I had gotten home Shelly hadn't made any fuss at all about my being out late. No repercussions from the law, none from my wife . . .

But the most surprising thing of all was that I found I could live with it. My sleep had certainly been sound enough. Any discomfort I felt this morning was due entirely to last night's drinking. That two women were dead was . . . well, it was just an unfortunate accident. There was nothing Ruskin and I could have done. Reporting the accident would have only gotten us in trouble. Besides, it wasn't as if they were happy young coeds with all their lives ahead of them. . . .

Vicki Kimberly came in and placed a letter on my desk. I scrawled my signature after a cursory glance.

"Jeez, you don't look so good today, Charley."

I smiled ruefully. "Little hung over, I'm afraid."

She giggled, as if I'd said something funny. I watched her leave, noting the way her beige skirt clung tightly to her hips. Nice. Very nice.

I remembered how I had danced with that woman last night, and the way I had desired her. I had always been a straight arrow with Shelly, but there I was ready to go to bed with that woman. I wondered if I would have felt any guilt had I done so. What was that woman's name? Amanda?

I pushed the memory way back into a cubbyhole and closed the door tight. The less I thought about that the better.

And, perhaps, the less I saw of Ruskin Marsh the better. He liked the fast lane a little too much for my taste. Last night had come perilously close to disaster, and I was in no mood to press my luck any further.

I reached into my In basket.

A month went by with a snap of the fingers, a month like any other except for one thing. A body had been found in one of the nearby valleys, one that fronted the eastern boundary of Mesa Vista. Only three blocks from my home, in fact. It was an illegal alien, and he had been robbed and murdered.

In the great flight of Mexicans to the United States, there were some who guided the illegals from Tijuana to America—and also preyed upon them. Murders were unfortunate but common; except, of course, for this particular one's proximity to Mesa Vista.

So, except for that, it was a fast month. Then Shelly told me there was to be a party on the upcoming Saturday at the Hart-fellens. The Marshes were invited so that they might be presented to Mesa Vista society, such as it was.

At the mention of Ruskin's name I was surprised to find that I was pleased. My reasons for not wanting to talk with him any-more now seemed indistinct and hazy, and perhaps, a little too hasty. Maybe I had made too much out of that evening.

And the past month had been a dry and colorless one indeed. I looked forward to seeing Ruskin again.

Burt Hartfellen worked at the Convair Division of General Dynamics. He was a project manager on the cruise missile con-tract, working on some facet of that operation that he wouldn't talk about. And business must have been fairly good, for his house was the biggest that was available—the "Conquistador" model, with five bedrooms and four baths—and he had recently installed a small pool in his backyard.

It was a ten-minute walk to their front door. The buzzer set off melodious chimes behind the custom mahogany door, and Dora Hartfellen, a sharp-featured woman in her late forties, ushered us in.

It was still early and I thought we would be the first guests, but standing in the entranceway were the Marshes, shaking hands and getting names straight with Burt. My hand disappeared into Burt's huge, calloused paw—he was a short but massively muscled man, brown as a walnut.

Then the doorbell bonged again and I turned to see the new arrivals. It was a teenage boy, tall and lanky and wearing a letter jacket, and he mumbled something to Dora about being there to pick up Debbie. Dora smiled and turned in the general direction of the stairs and bellowed for her daughter. Burt went over and shook the boy's hand, and I could see from the boy's expression it was Burt's standard knuckle-buster.

Debbie Hartfellen came thumping down the stairs and breezed on by. She had almost made a clean getaway with her date when Dora stopped her, turned her around, and made her come back to be introduced to her guests. Debbie did this in the sullen, sulky sort of way reserved for meeting such nonpersons as adults.

Sixteen or seventeen, she was the sort of girl I remembered having heated fantasies about in high school. She was fully and ripely developed, so much so that she seemed more a caricature of a sex bomb than a human girl. My wife's gossip had it that Debbie was a rebellious sort, and that she and her mother were often at odds.

I shook her hand gravely, noting that her makeup did indeed make her look a little bit like a slut. But perhaps it was just awkwardness with handling cosmetics, for I thought I detected something else there. An uncertainty. A shyness.

She shook hands with Ruskin and Sybil, her voice dull and totally uninterested, then she was out the door with her boyfriend.

Burt ushered Ruskin and me out back. A bar was set up by the swimming pool, and four tiki-tiki torches cast a wavering glow. Stars were beginning to dust the sky, and Venus was losing its prominence. He asked for drink orders, then broke the tax seal on a bottle of good bourbon. Burt raised his thick eyebrows darkly. "Hell of a thing about that Mexican, isn't it?"

"Sybil actually saw it," Ruskin said. "She was driving by when they were bringing the body up out of the canyon. Gave her quite a start."

"I saw a little bit of it on television," I said. "A shot from one of the news helicopters. Even saw a little bit of my own house. Hope this doesn't mean more of them are going to get killed round here."

"That's not what worries me," Burt said. He stopped pouring, bottle poised over a thick glass. "Heard something strange about it. Goddamn peculiar, really. They say the Mexican had been tortured." He gave Ruskin and me a quick glance. "Whoever did it also cut off his *balls*."

"Jesus," I said quietly. I took one of the finished drinks and had a big knock. It was a ghastly bit of news, but still well within the bounds of recent experience. Perhaps he had been a rival to one of the other guides, had stepped into someone else's territory. I heard the double bong of the front door, then the muted sounds of greeting and laughter.

"Excuse me, guys," Burt said. "Time to meet the new batch."

He went off, leaving Ruskin and me alone.

"Burt seems like an interesting guy," Ruskin said. "And his daughter . . . juicy little item, isn't she?"

He chuckled good-naturedly. I laughed a little, too. I thought about asking him if he'd heard anything more about that night with the pickups from the restaurant. Discarded it. The less said about that the better. I searched for another subject.

"Hope that dead body didn't upset your wife," I said.

He shook his head. "Believe me, we had more than our share of grisly incidents up in San Francisco. In fact, we lived right next to a park where a lot of weird stuff went on." He laughed softly at some memory. "Why, one fine day the police found these two fifty-gallon drums in the bushes—"

"I don't know if I want to hear this."

Hint of a grin. "—and it turned out there were three bodies in those drums. A man in one, two women in the other. They'd been shot. But later the coroner said the bullets weren't the cause of death. Just icing on the cake, actually. You see, they'd been worked over with a blowtorch." He sipped his drink and shrugged. "Turned out they were prostitutes. Some kind of revenge thing."

"Revenge," I mouthed quietly.

He turned to me and I saw that for a man with such dark hair his eyes were incredibly blue. It made me think of the diamond-edged tips of industrial drill bits. "Maybe it wasn't revenge," he said quietly, almost soothingly. "Maybe they were killed just for fun. Some people get off on that, don't they?"

"I can't imagine that." The tiki-tiki torches cast writhing shadows against the pool's deck. It framed Ruskin like that famous self-portrait of Van Gogh, the one where the background is billowing sworls of blue-green. My mouth felt suddenly dry and cottony, and I took a quick sip of my drink. "I can't imagine that someone would kill simply for pleasure."

Ruskin looked back to the house, chuckling. "Oh, no?"

The dark of full evening was almost upon Mesa Vista. It crept behind the tiki-tiki torches, biding its time, knowing that it would soon have full sway. I felt uneasy. I had looked forward to talking with Ruskin, but now I felt an urge to be with other people. "C'mon. Let me introduce you to the local crowd."

The first one we met was Al Goodweather, a tall, shambling man who had changed much in the few months I'd known him. A little shy and reserved to begin with, he was so painfully silent nowadays I was surprised he'd shown up tonight. There were dark circles under his eyes.

"Al's with Infidex," I said as Ruskin pumped his hand. "He's in charge of software development."

"Infidex?" Ruskin said. "Didn't they just lay off a couple hundred people?"

Al's shoulders seemed to slump a little more. "Right."

I raced for something to change the subject. It was well known that Infidex was on the greasy skids, and this more than likely had everything to do with Al's chronic depression. But before I could say anything, Shelly was tugging at my elbow, begging me to come take a look at the Hartfellens' latest toy.

So I left them and went off with my wife. The toy turned out to be one of those huge television sets, the kind with the six-foot-wide screen. They had it hooked up with their Atari, and electronic invaders from space were surprisingly gigantic on the wide screen. A joy stick was pressed in my hand, and I quickly became wrapped up in the game.

It was a new kind of icebreaker. A crowd of people stood around and shouted encouragement. I beat old Fred Galloway hands down, and his eager replacement was Sarah Weinburner, saucy young wife of a guy who worked for Cubic. I worked the joy stick frantically, giving little cries of "shit!" and "hah!" But Sarah was intent, and with a maddeningly girlish giggle zapped my last man. I handed the controls over to Bill Terrace and got up.

I was surprised at how sweat had beaded my forehead. Alcoholic refreshment seemed in order. As I headed back to the bar, I was surprised to see Ruskin and Al Goodweather by themselves in a corner, still deep in conversation. What on earth had they been talking about for so long?

It was fully dark outside, the only illumination being the torches and the bright blue glow from the pool's underwater lights. A couple sat at the pool's apron, the woman slowly swashing her hand in the water and making wriggling shadows dance across the backside of the house. I poured a glass of Coke, slopped in some rum, and drank it thirstily.

I headed for the kitchen, a place where there is usually convivial company in any party. But it was dark and unused in there, except for a soft yellow glow from underneath the up-slung microwave. I had almost flicked on the bright fluorescents when I saw a couple in the corner. It was Sarah Weinburner and Jack Burnett, slowly grinding against each other and working on a meaty kiss. I backed out and walked away, feeling foolish. I hoped Jack knew what he was doing. Sarah's husband Ralph had once played pro ball with the Chargers.

I looked around for Ruskin but did not see him. Sybil was on prominent display, however. She was the center of attention of a small group of men, all clustered around her and grinning like horny jackasses. Sybil smiled and posed, occasionally favoring one with a laugh at his joke or a touch upon his shoulder. She was fantastically exotic and beautiful, by far the most attractive woman at the party. Belle of the ball, suburban style.

I spotted Al Goodweather sitting in a corner by himself. He

was leaning forward, his long arms draped over his knees, the expression on his face slack and drawn. If anyone needed cheering up, it was he. I walked over, guts warm with booze, feeling magnanimous.

"Hello, Al." I sat beside him and gave him a slap on the back. "Hear the one about the three gays in a hot tub?"

But Al took no notice of me. All he did was start leaning even farther forward, his big bony hands slowly coming up to meet his face. I suddenly knew what was going to happen, and all I could do was sit there and watch it.

His face met his hands and his back began heaving and shuddering. The stereo was loud with a Jobim record, but I could still hear Al's sobbing.

"Hey . . ." I felt completely helpless. What can you do? "Al, man, hey. It's all right."

This did nothing but make him cry all the harder. It was ghastly.

My first thought was to get him out of the living room, away from people. If I were in his position . . . well, I'd want some privacy. "C'mon, Al." I helped him up. "Let's get out of here, fella."

A high, snickering sob escaped from his hands, making some people turn their heads. I opened the first door that came to hand, and led him into Burt's lavishly appointed home business office. I was just about to shut the door when Al's wife came in and shut it for me. Relief flooded through me.

Sheri Goodweather was a level-headed woman, quite attractive in an outdoorsy sort of way. But now her face was as wide and strained and horrified as if she were watching her home slide into a fissure. "Al, honey? Darling?" She went to him and I was glad to get out of the way. I'll never forget that look of desperate puzzlement. "Christ, darling, what is it?"

Al sank into the Naugahyde loveseat, head still buried in his hands, still racked with that gruesome sobbing. Sheri wrapped her arms around him and began whispering urgently. Al was a big man, but now he looked more like Sheri's child than her husband. It was a sad little spectacle.

I asked Sheri if I could do anything. She shook her head without looking at me and I quietly opened the door and went out.

I leaned against the door and sighed. I didn't know what to

make of it. I didn't know if I wanted to make anything of it. I walked toward the poolside bar, a little stiff-legged.

The bulk of the party had moved out here. I went up to the bar and helped myself to some Jim Beam, straight. People chatted in groups, elaborately casual, but I sensed a certain tension in the air, a certain anticipation. But of what?

There was a deep, booming splash and then the sizzling of water spraying on the concrete apron. Some laughter and shrieks. I saw an underwater figure shooting forward, the shape unmistakably and gloriously female. She broke surface and stood, pushing the slickered hair from her face, perfect bosom wobbling proud and free. It was Sybil Marsh.

There were more splashes, more shrieks of laughter. Skinny-dipping time. So this was the kind of party it was going to be. A first for Mesa Vista.

I began unbuttoning my shirt, the effort seeming like an overly finicky chore. The last button sort of popped off, and I went into the pool cannonball-style.

It was cool but not cold. I stood, feeling much soberized. Sarah Weinburner swam by, sleek as an otter and quite lovely. She saw me and smiled, then hooked around toward me. She stopped herself by hooking one arm around my waist, then draped her other arm over my shoulder and hiked herself up. Her big, wet breasts squished against me as she took my tongue in her mouth, and I could feel the vibration of her "umm" against my teeth. I clung on to her mightily, wishing it was Sybil. Then she unlocked herself and swam away, laughing like a mermaid, leaving me with the beginnings of an erection.

I began swimming. About half the party goers were stripped, the others looking on and laughing. I saw Burt Hartfellen by the poolside, hands on hips, chuckling like a merry, burly Bacchus.

But bacchanal it was not to be. There was some kissing and feeling up going on, but that looked as far as it was going to get. Most of the activity seemed to be a sort of lazy play with a basketball and other Hartfellen pool toys.

Someone got me from behind, wrapping her arms around my shoulders. It was Shelly, strands of wet blond hair half covering her face. "Hello, stranger."

"Fancy meeting you here."

We grinned at each other, two slightly embarrassed people looking for something to say. Then Shelly suddenly seemed conscious of her nakedness. "I think I've had enough."

"I'm going to stay in a little more." As if I were calling to say I was going to play another nine holes and would be late.

"I'll be inside," she called, swimming away. I watched her get out, studying the small roll of fat at her belly. It had really almost disappeared. The increased tempo of visits to the Family Fitness Center was evidently doing some good.

I swam a little more, no longer interested in finding Sybil. I was surprised at how quickly I was becoming used to everyone's nudity. The ball came my way and I bounced it back, laughing as if I were having fun.

I got out and went to the Jacuzzi, was pleased when I saw Ruskin chest-high in the swirling foam. I got in. "Been looking for you Ruskin, my man."

He grinned at me in a pleasant, drunk sort of way. "Charles . . ." He had both his arms spread on the Jacuzzi's rim, and next to him, leaning her head against his shoulder, was good old Sarah Weinburner. She smiled at me, eyes half-closed and glossed over. She looked on the verge of passing out.

I searched for something to say. "So now what do you think of our friendly little neighborhood?"

He turned to Sarah and grinned down at her. "I'd say I was going to like it here fine. It's a place where a man can set down roots." Sarah gave a throaty chuckle.

"You and Al seemed to hit it off," I said. "What were you two talking about?"

He turned to me and shrugged indifferently. "Things."

"Like what?"

"Like if you have any stock in Infidex, now's the time to dump it."

I nodded, then noticed something that should have been apparent when I first got in the Jacuzzi. The angle of Sarah's arm, the way her shoulder muscle was working . . . she was giving Ruskin a leisurely hand job underneath the sizzling foam.

I got out of the Jacuzzi without excusing myself, went over

to where I had thrown my clothes. Draped around the pool-side furniture were several big towels, courtesy of Dora Hartfellen, the compleat hostess. I toweled myself dry and got dressed. As I snapped on the Seiko, I saw that it was eleven-thirty. Time had gone fast. I went back in the house, searching for coffee.

But before I got to the kitchen, I saw that the front door was wide open. I went to close it, then saw a small group standing on the front walk. I went outside.

It was Al Goodweather, shoulders slumped and still sobbing, supported on one side by Burt Hartfellen and on the other by Sheri Goodweather. My feet crunched gravel and Sheri turned and looked at me, horribly embarrassed.

"How's he doing?" I asked softly.

"He won't stop crying. I don't know what's happening to him."

"Here it comes," Burt said, pointing down the street. It was one of those big boxy ambulances the paramedics use. "Good, they kept the siren off." Burt began ushering Al to the curb, Sheri assisting. I stood and watched.

Some other curiosity seeker came out of the house. It was Jean Waggoner, an attractive woman a little older than I. We had always gotten along very well in a comfortable brother-sister type of relationship.

"Charles," she whispered, "what the hell is going on?"

I quickly filled her in, her eyes growing wider with each word.

The ambulance pulled up and stopped, and while the motor was still idling, a white-jacketed man got out of the cab and swung open the rear doors. The ambulance's radio was on very loud, the monotonous drones of the dispatcher and hissing of static echoing off the nearby houses. Al got in slowly, like an old man, still blubbering. Then Burt helped Sheri step inside. I saw Al lay on a stretcher, and Sheri took a seat beside him. The double doors huffed closed. The ambulance took off at the posted speed limit of twenty-five, taking its electronic squeaks and squawks with it.

Burt watched the ambulance round the Fitzaddams' house and disappear. He came back up the walkway, acknowledged Jean's presence with a quick nod. "Sheri told me Al lost his job day before yesterday," Burt said. "He's been quiet ever since. Up until tonight, that is."

I told Burt how Al had started breaking down with me. Burt shook his head. "Then he's been crying for two solid hours. Jesus. Hope there's some shrink on duty at the hospital tonight. C'mon, you two. We need drinks."

We went back to the house. No one seemed to have noticed the little incident outside, and Burt was visibly relieved. There was still some skinny-dipping going on, but it was winding down. Someone called Burt, and he left Jean and me to ourselves.

"Some party," I said.

Jean frowned, making her look like a stern schoolmarm. "It stinks, Charles. It's all wrong. This isn't the kind of party good neighborhoods have."

"You feel that strongly about a little bare-assed swimming?"

She looked at me and smiled. "I'm no prude. But ... there's something terribly wrong here tonight. Something ... oh, I don't know."

There was a sudden scream. Jean tensed up abruptly, almost comically. I had seen something like this when I was in the Navy, while the *Groves* was qualifying on the gunnery range: when the first salvo of the day snapped off, everybody but everybody gave this same tense jerk as their relaxed nervous systems came to grips with the startling shock of the five-inch batteries report. That was how Jean reacted, and I guess I did, too.

The commotion was coming from out back, from somewhere near the Jacuzzi. Jean and I hurried to the big sliding glass doors, and there we stopped. Or maybe it would be more accurate to say we froze.

Two men were fighting. One was Ralph Weinburner, husband of the often-straying Sarah. The other was Ruskin Marsh, who was, incredibly, buck naked. Sarah herself was still in the Jacuzzi, hands clapped over her mouth, her first shriek evidently being her last.

It was something you dread to see at any party, the worst of all possible scenes. Ruskin's nudity added a ghastly, grotesque touch.

Ralph Weinburner was built like a tank, and his big moon face was contorted with a killer's fury. He swung wild haymakers, backing Ruskin off the Jacuzzi deck. Ruskin was crouched in the classic fighter's pose, head lowered, fists raised, shoulders waggling as he feinted and jabbed and probed for an opening. Ruskin was intent, and as far as I could tell, totally unconcerned with his nakedness.

I left Jean and started toward the fight. I saw Burt Hartfellen running in from the far side of the pool. Other men were beginning to move toward the fight.

Just before Burt got there, I saw Ruskin find his opening. The blows went in one, two, three, like a blur. Ralph dropped his forearms to his midsection, and Ruskin snapped a right into Ralph's big, meaty throat. Ralph sank to his knees, gagging, eyes wide.

That should have been it, but Ruskin grabbed Ralph's shoulders, and bracing himself, jammed his knee up and into Ralph's jaw. Ralph's head bounced backward, and I heard a horrible little *snap*. Ralph collapsed on his back, arms splayed wide, just as Burt and I and everyone else reached them.

And still Ruskin was not done. He was preparing to lunge upon Ralph when Burt grabbed his arm and held him back, then Don Fisher got his other arm. Ruskin twisted and tried to pull away, his eyes bright and intense and glued to the gasping form of Ralph Weinburner, his lips drawn back in a snarl.

Seven

The party was the topic of neighborhood conversation for quite some time.

Ruskin had broken Ralph's jaw. For some while there was talk of charges being filed, though none ever were. Shelly's grapevine had it that Ralph and Sarah Weinburner were negotiating a separation.

This same grapevine had all the juicy details on Al Goodweather, too. Evidently he had cried all the way to the hospital, cried in the emergency room, cried when they slid a needle in his arm and gave him a dose of Thorazine, and kept on crying until they gave him a bigger dose. One week later Sheri Goodweather was gone for good, she and her two kids having moved in with her parents in Minnesota. Al did not go with them. They say that Al did not know who Sheri was anymore. Al was institutionalized in a not very nice place, the kind that's exposed on "60 Minutes" as having scrimped in the patient-care department.

I thought about that party much longer than I should have, enough so that I found it difficult to concentrate on work. Scenes kept drifting through my mind, disconnected and without any logic. Sybil Marsh diving naked into the pool. Garish video blips marching across a gigantic television screen. Burt telling me the Mexican had been castrated. Al gently weeping into his huge, bony hands. Ruskin glaring at the recumbent form of Ralph with a baleful, demonic intensity.

It was like a mobile hung too high to reach. I wanted to wrestle it down and make it make some kind of sense. But all I had was a gut reaction, which was that it had all the appeal of a run-over skunk in the middle of July. And as for Ruskin, well, I wondered how the party might have turned out had the Marshes not come. Maybe there wouldn't have been a fight. Any other man would have been more circumspect in taking liberties with Sarah Weinburner, and thus have avoided an ugly showdown with Ralph.

And that thing with Al Goodweather. He had obviously been on the verge of a breakdown, but it was peculiar that he had not really gone off the deep end until after his little talk with Ruskin.

I wondered if that meant anything. I wondered if Al might have been given a little shove, somehow. But even if that were so, why would Ruskin have done it? Fun?

I thought of what Ruskin had said about those grisly murders in San Francisco, the ones that were done with a blowtorch. I thought of the way Ruskin had stared at me as the tiki-tiki torches cast their wavering glow.

Maybe they did it just for fun. Some people get off on that, don't they?

I thought about that a lot. And of that expression on Ruskin's face as he was being held back from killing Ralph.

Fun.

Perhaps I'd better cool things with Ruskin. There was something dark and unsavory about that man, something that filled me with a vague unease.

"Mr. Ripley? Charley?"

It was Vicki Kimberly, and even though she was standing in front of my desk, it startled me. "What is it?"

"Mr. Anderson's just called a staff meeting. He wants all of you guys in the conference room right away."

"Oh. Okay. Thanks." I picked up a yellow pad as I got out of my chair.

The crisis was that Aerotel had lost some time and gone way over budget on a project that everyone (myself included) said related to themselves only distantly. A rumor had it that a surprise audit was due any day from the Department of Defense.

The tempo of work immediately surged to emergency alert status. People stayed late without being asked, in order to review files.

The crisis quickly gobbled up the week, and I found myself not only putting in a full day Saturday but also a half-day Sunday. By the time the surprise audit came, most everyone's ducks were in neat-enough rows. The main office came up squeaky clean, and DoD was satisfied with the sacrificial lambs offered up from Aerotel's production facility out at the other end of the county.

It had been exhausting, and not very much fun. Time had gone fast, it was true; but whereas once I had thrived on such a crisis, now it seemed merely wearying. But that was my lot, I thought. That was the way my life was. Make the best of it. At least *try* and enjoy it.

So, on a weekend two weeks after the party, I threw myself into a new routine. I was the Upright Suburbanite, I told myself. A working joe—a *content* working joe, I quickly amended—in the booming, important aerospace industry, owner of a fine home, husband of a wife with an almost-flat belly, pursuer of interesting hobbies, a relentless marcher toward the well-planned Golden Years. The only thing that should have concerned me was whether Shelly and I should adopt a child—and not the meaningless dust motes of paintings and books and other gibberish.

I attended to my bookcase project. Saturday I went out to Handyman and bought the rest of the wood I needed. I spent the evening puttering around the spare bedroom. Or study, rather. I had furnished it with various cast-offs from the rest of the house, and the only thing that was really needed was the bookcase itself. I straightened the pile of books into neat stacks, and was a little surprised when I came across the book Ruskin had loaned me. I had completely forgotten about it. But before I could open it, Shelly called me to dinner.

Much later that night Shelly and I made love in the Jacuzzi. I found myself making the right noises and correct moves, but my mind was elsewhere. I thought about the book, and wondered why Ruskin hadn't asked for it back. I thought about the day he had given it to me, and of the things that had happened on that rainy night.

And with Shelly astride me and the Jacuzzi foam churning warmly around I looked at her blissful face and thought of another one. One that belonged to a body in flames, staggering in the damp night, clawing helplessly.

I began losing my erection, and even though I hadn't, I told Shelly that I had come.

I awoke early Sunday even though I had spent a restless night. I threw myself into the bookcase project, carefully measuring each board and penciling in where I would cut. I was so wrapped up I barely noticed Shelly taking off around noon to go with Sybil to the fitness center. I was having fun, you see. Good, clean, wholesome fun. Definitely not the type Ruskin had been talking about.

I thought about how I had wanted to be his friend, and forced a laugh. Imagine me, a grown man, wanting to waste time talking about ... whatever. Hadn't I gotten my fill of that in college? I forced another laugh.

I put a piece of wood on the workbench and set it flush with the dog blocks. I picked up the circular saw and set it on the penciled line. I tensed up, preparing for the loud noise of the power saw.

Loneliness. What right did I have to worry about that? That was something for pimply high school kids to moon over. My life was full to the brim.

I squeezed the on/off button and the machine wanged and clattered and the noise slammed off the cinder block walls. I pushed the saw along the penciled line, little piles of sawdust dancing atop the vibrating wood.

I reached the end of the line and the wood snapped in two. I released the on/off trigger and the silence rang loudly in my ears.

I felt restless Sunday night, but couldn't put my finger on why. I went into the living room to see if there was anything good on television, but Shelly was in her exercise togs, doggedly following the instructions of *Jane Fonda's Workout* videocassette. I watched the little portable in the kitchen, but all "Masterpiece Theatre" had on was something about this veterinarian, and the stuff on the other channels was even worse. I thought about tomorrow being Monday, and felt even more restless.

I settled down in my study, a glass of wine handy. The cheap but nice-looking canvas chair was comfortable. I turned on the cutesy brass reading lamp Shelly had bought at Pier One.

Juliette, by the Marquis de Sade. I had heard of him, of course. Who hadn't? But I had never read anything by him.

Kinky sex. I thought of the many porno magazines and fuck books I had read in my Navy days, the back pages of which always contained a few ads for articles to assist in sadistic acts. These were invariably small little ads, the pictures and text so crudely put together they looked as if they were laid out on a kitchen table.

I had even seen an S&M movie once, a little 8mm job some bearded and grinning warrant officer had shown me shortly after I reported aboard the U.S.S. *Groves*. Its technical quality approached that of the magazine ads. I remembered a skinny, tattooed man strapped to a motel bed, hiding his face from the harsh lights as a plump, young flooze giggled and shrugged at the camera, obviously asking the director what she was supposed to be doing with the phony whip.

But this, *Juliette or the Fortunes of Vice*—this was the grandaddy of them all. I turned over the title page. The next page was blank; there was no publication date. Indeed, no publishing house was listed at all. I turned to the first chapter and began reading.

It was written in that slow, plodding style all old books I have ever looked at are written in. I was reminded of interminable afternoons in a high school classroom, listening to some old biddy explain the themes in *Silas Marner* or *Wuthering Heights*. For me, de Sade had come up to the plate with two strikes against him.

Bored, I leafed ahead, scanning the pages. Then I struck on an exchange between Juliette and a minister of the French government. He tells Juliette he has had her parents poisoned. Her reply: "Your confession that you are a murderer inflames me and makes me burningly passionate." They have some kinky sex. Then he enlists her to poison his rivals, giving her thirty thousand per murder. Source of this money? The government agency he controls. "A statesman would be a fool if he did not let his country pay for his pleasures. What matters to us the misery of the people if only our passions are satisfied? If I thought that gold might flow from the veins of people, I would have them blood-let one after the other, that I might cover myself in their gore."

I backtracked and began reading more carefully. The first acts were relatively innocuous. Children were seduced. There were orgies between monks and nuns. Entire families were forced to perform incest with one another. Juliette meets up with Pope Pius VI, and together they celebrate a black mass, then retire to St. Peter's Basilica for an orgy.

The book picked up steam. I read a long and loving descrip-
tion of an orgy wherein the main diversion was the torture of
a young maiden. And when she finally expired, the corpse was
gang-banged. I closed the book, dinner now a hard and undi-
gested knot.

I left my study and went back into the bright and clean
twentieth century, to white wine and a rerun of "The Tonight
Show."

But I couldn't block recollections of what I had read. Much
later that night I lay in bed uneasily, my mind slipping in and out
of sleep. One moment I was warm on the still waterbed, the only
sound my wife's steady breathing, and then a nonsensical and
repulsive horror would float up from my subconscious.

Despite the bad dreams, despite the occasional nausea, on the
following days I could not put down the book. It was perversely
engrossing. I told myself it was the same emotion all of us felt
when we heard the carnival barker sing out tales of reptilian
women and two-headed fetuses, a call that made you want to
draw back the curtain and go inside the dark, crowded tent.

But in the middle of the book de Sade began repeating himself. Juliette and her friends had gotten to the point where murder
was their chief pleasure. Having arrived at that, de Sade sought to
compound it. During one "performance" at the Theatre of Horrors, 1,176 people were executed on stage, and brutally so. One
of Juliette's friends set fire to thirty-seven hospitals in Rome and
some twenty thousand people were burnt to death.

I looked ahead and the rest of the book seemed to be more of
the same. So murder was it. That was where de Sade's intellect
had finally found sanctuary.

I found the book interesting because it represented what could
happen if a person let his mind go all the way. True, de Sade had
been some kind of psychopath and his mind had gone down
some truly gruesome corridors . . . but I had at least one thing to
say to his good: He had taken his mind to the outermost limit of
his senses. He had let nothing—no moral, no ethic, no convention—dissuade him from his purpose. He had stood on his own
two feet and let the chips fall where they may. Like some kind of

depraved John Wayne. I smiled at my analogy. Then frowned in thought.

John Wayne, maybe. Ruskin Marsh . . . that was rather more like it.

Saturday rolled around and I puttered in the garage/workshop. Sybil came by about nine or so and picked up Shelly. One of the shelves wouldn't fit in just right, and I ended up putting a dandy little scratch on the inside of the bookcase. It made me angry out of all proportion to the incident. Noon came and my stomach started rumbling.

I went in and made myself a ham-and-sprout sandwich and popped open an Oly. I ate and drank quickly, standing at the counter with sweat and sawdust on my forearms. I slowed down on the eating and strolled into my study.

Maybe I should just break down and *buy* a goddamn bookcase. I leaned over and picked up *Juliette*, careful not to get my greasy hands on its pages. It had been a few days since I'd lost interest in the book, and quite some time since Ruskin had loaned it. The AM/FM on my desk said it was twelve-thirty. I decided I would pay Ruskin a quick visit. Return the book. Maybe talk a little, if he had some time.

I walked out back and saw that Ruskin wasn't working in his yard. I stepped over the low fence that separated our backyards, then hopped up the two steps that led to his back patio. I walked to the sliding glass door, hand ready to knock. I froze like an animal caught in headlights, staring into the living room.

It was Ruskin and young Miss Debbie Hartfellen, naked and in the final frenzy of some on-the-floor sex. I stood there like a statue, mouth wide, utterly unable to move. Ruskin was kneeling behind her, hands on her firm young derriere. He was thrusting and circling his hips, eyes open but rolled back so far only the whites showed. Debbie had her hands on the floor, mouth wide with a silent gasp. Her big, doughy breasts wobbled back and forth as Ruskin worked against her. Some clothes were scattered around—bright red jogging shorts, Ruskin's cutoffs, T-shirts. I could hear Ruskin begin to gasp, digging his hands into her thighs and completely pulling her legs up off the floor.

Three seconds passed before I finally found the connections that made me walk quietly backward. I stepped off the patio and strode back to my fence.

I went inside the house and walked to the kitchen. I put the unreturned book on the counter and pulled out a fresh Oly. Half went down on the first swig.

"*Jesus,*" I said out loud. "Son of a *bitch!*"

I was sure I hadn't been seen. They were too far gone for that. I shook my head as I reran the little scene, not knowing what to make of it.

Christ help Ruskin if Burt Hartfellen found out. Or the California Bar, for that matter. The age of consent in California was eighteen, and Debbie was at least a full year from that. And Debbie did not strike me as the soul of discretion.

It was horrible and stupid, and yet . . . I could not deny that something was making me smile about it, as if it were a droll little episode from a Baroque farce. Debbie Hartfellen, the ripe young maiden. Ruskin the lucky satyr.

How many men in this neighborhood had lusted after Debbie? Had I? Well, perhaps in an abstract way, only insofar as she was the quintessence of California beach bunny beauty . . . but never had I looked upon her and wished that we could have sex. Or at least not to the extent that I would take even the first step in bringing that plan to fruition.

I drained the beer and got another. How had Ruskin done it? Met her jogging? Debbie jogged frequently, as every man in Mesa Vista knew.

Well, Shelly was right about one thing. Debbie was indeed something of a slut.

I lifted the beer can high, letting the icy cold splash down my throat. None of it was any of my business. I would think of it no more.

But late that night, as I lay on the still waterbed, I kept thinking of Debbie standing in the hallway of her parents' house, sullen and sulky as she was being introduced to the grown-ups. I remembered that close up her makeup did not look so much whorish as just awkwardly put on. And then, as I slipped into the first taste of unconsciousness, there came the face of Ruskin Marsh, contorted and strained as he approached his orgasm, eyes rolled back so that the sockets contained only two white orbs.

I woke late Sunday. Once breakfast was done I went into the garage and looked at the bookcase. It wasn't even half done. Well, I'd give it one more try.

Sybil Marsh walked over, her electric-blue bodysuit positively glimmering in the bright sunlight. In addition to her designer gym bag, she carried the Black & Decker lawn trimmer I'd loaned Ruskin. She came into the garage, the bodysuit losing its sheen but grin still maintaining its hundred-watt glow. "Ruskin said to drop this by."

"Thanks." I took it and hung it on the stud. "Coming by to pick up Shelly?"

"Yep."

"I'll walk you inside. I want to return something I borrowed from Ruskin."

We went in and I saw Shelly had already dressed up for their afternoon workout. Funny she hadn't mentioned her plans to me. I went to the living room and picked up *Juliette*. When I handed it over, Sybil's face brightened in recognition. "Oh, so you're the one who had it. Did you enjoy it?"

I shrugged. "It was okay." Actually, it was only half read. Sybil slipped it in her gym bag. I watched the women leave. They were giggling at something.

Eight

Debbie ran away two weeks later. Shelly told me the last the Hartfellens heard was a letter from Debbie saying she couldn't take it anymore, that she was going off to Los Angeles to make it as a big model. Or maybe as an actress. Burt was rumored to have hired a private investigator.

"Poor Dora," Shelly said. "She's on the verge of a breakdown. It's awful." She took a sip of her wine. We were eating pork chops, a food that I did not care for, as I had told Shelly time and again. "Can you imagine what's happening to that child in Los Angeles?"

"Nothing good, I'm sure." I wondered if Ruskin had anything to do with it. Discarded it. It was silly. Debbie was just another dumb, promiscuous girl. After all, prostitutes had to come from *somewhere*. I brought the napkin to my mouth, hiding my smile from Shelly.

"Still, I can see how Dora brought it on herself," Shelly said. "She was always so strict with that girl, always criticizing her. And, well, you know Debbie."

"Know what?"

She looked me in the eyes. "You know what I mean. Whenever she jogged by, every man in this neighborhood would have their tongues hanging out."

I spread my hands. "C'mon!"

She looked down at her plate and shrugged. "She just looked a little on the trashy side." She looked at me suddenly and grinned. "Guess I'm getting older. Criticizing a young hussy."

Yeah, sounded like that to me, too. "You're not getting older, Shelly."

"Just better? Thank you, sir." She pushed at her food listlessly. She seemed on the verge of saying something, then let out this big, wearying sigh.

I took her hand in mine. "Let's go out to the Jacuzz, darling. Let's get naked."

She gave a bright smile and nodded. I grinned back, trying to place her expression. Then it came to me. It was the brave-little-soldier smile, the kind a good girl wears when she's getting ready to receive a shot.

We made love in the swirling water, in darkness, the only sounds the occasional car passing by out front and the whirr of the water pump. Like the last time, there was no excitement. And I sensed it was the same for Shelly.

When we finished we lay back and drank wine, looking at the few stars that were visible. Then, without speaking, Shelly got up and quickly wrapped herself in a terry-cloth robe. She said she was going to bed and I said I was going to stay out a little longer.

I leaned my head against the tub's lip, trying to pick out a constellation. Way out in the Pacific you can see billions upon billions of stars hanging in the black velvet, the Milky Way a long, loose scattering of dust. Here the smog and the lights of the city blocked out all but the brightest.

From next door came the muffled sound of Ruskin and Sybil laughing. Then Mark's high-pitched giggling. I looked at their house but could only see the lights on behind a few windows, shades and drapes drawn. I took another sip of wine.

I was lonesome. God, so terribly lonesome.

I got out of the tub but did not pick up the towel. Naked and dripping, I walked to the back of my property and looked at the opposite ridge. There were a few lights on at Viewscape Estates. I looked down into the canyon. Brother, was it ever dark down there. I wondered if there were any Mexicans running around, if perhaps another one was being killed even as I looked into the still, inky void.

It was strange standing there naked, and yet kind of exciting. I looked back over my shoulder at the score of houses within my field of view. I felt an urge to go running through the neighborhood naked, hiding and darting, seeing how long I could keep it up before someone would call the cops.

I looked back into the valley. And when the police were after me I'd run down there, into the darkness, a wild man, laughing.

I felt a powerful urge to do it, and knew not whence it came.

But it was there, and it seemed all I could do to hold myself still and not go scampering off nude throughout Mesa Vista Estates. The inside of my chest tingled with excitement. Blood flowed down to my penis and I became turgidly erect. The valley below seemed alive with horrors, with the evil things de Sade had written about, with Ruskin thrusting himself into Debbie, eyes no longer eyes, but things that were blankly white. And, standing there, I began to masturbate. Three tugs and I came so that my knees felt ready to give way.

Nine

"This is it." Vicki Kimberly waved her hand as she walked into the tiny living room. "My little pride and joy. Or half of it anyway, if you count a roommate."

I shut the door as I walked in. "Nice. Charming. Close to work, too."

"Yeah." She tossed her shoulder bag on a bright yellow bean bag chair. The small room was dominated by two old double-hung windows, through which soft, shaded sunlight and street noise flowed in. One story below was Fifth Street, which for two blocks was the main drag of Hillcrest, a pleasant neighborhood in its own right but still well within the city limits of San Diego. The Aerotel office was several blocks south on this same street, a distance of only about five minutes.

"So what's for lunch?" I asked. This was the little conceit Vicki maintained when she asked if she might return the luncheon treat. She had been evasive as to our destination right up until she put her key in the lock. In answer to my question she turned and laughed, as if in fond exasperation.

"Now do you really want to eat?" She advanced, chuckling with wholesome mirth. "Is that what you think I brought you up here for?"

Without further ado she wrapped her arms around my waist and squinted up at me, making me think this was an awkward but loving embrace between brother and sister. Some seduction. This was more like *Mr. Hobbs Takes a Mistress*.

We kissed, and instantly she switched from the nonsexual routine to that of the steamy, yearning-to-be-satisfied temptress. She clung and pressed against me fiercely, drawing down my head for a moaning, all-encompassing kiss. It seemed as if my neck were caught in a hammerlock. My knees slowly buckled and we went down together, still holding the kiss.

Frantic. We undressed each other frantically. Vicki had a

dazed, almost shocked look on her face. Maybe she had planned to maneuver us to the bedroom before the action began, but now that it was happening on the living room floor she was surprised but unwilling to stop. I breathed quickly as I rid her of the skirt, but it was not with building passion. I felt more like a desperate kid at Christmas, fearing that as I tore open the last present the thing that had been most wanted might not be there after all.

The moan of the first kiss still continued, at least on Vicki's part. She was deeply into it, and I had not seen such fervor since the first year of my marriage. We rolled in the cast-off clothes, gasping and clutching, and I feared it would turn out to be an act on my part, like the last few times with Shelly.

I soon found myself in the same position Ruskin had used with Debbie Hartfellen. Vicki continued with the moans, the muscles of her hard young ass pulling and contracting beneath my grip. She turned her profile to me and rolled her pink tongue across her lips, eyes closed in intense bliss.

"Harder, harder . . ."

A *Penthouse* fantasy come true. Yet there was nothing here but a certain frictive energy. Most of my mind was focused on the opposite wall, against which leaned a gleaming ten-speed. I could imagine Vicki astride it, zipping through the nearby park on a sunny day. A luscious, healthy young girl any man would give his right arm to be with in the same way I was now. I felt guilty that I wasn't having much fun. This wasn't anything like I'd thought it would be. Just like that stupid lunch I'd had with her. I was beginning to look forward to having done with it. I felt like an idiot.

Vicki's moans continued unabated, actually increasing in volume. It was driving me nuts. It sounded like I was *hurting* her, for Christ's sake. Angrily, I grabbed her hair and yanked hard, intent upon twisting her face around and demanding that she shut the fuck up.

"*Ughn . . .*" Her head turned as if to look over her shoulder. Her eyes fluttered halfway open and all I could see were the whites. "*Ughn, oh . . .*"

A sudden rush of power welled from deep within my gut, tingling the muscles in my legs and making my penis go from passably turgid to steel-hard. The breath left my lungs, replaced by a subzero cold. Not knowing why, I pulled her hair all the harder, drawing her head back at a painful angle. She closed her eyes tight and hissed through clamped teeth (*was this pain? was this pleasure?*) and I could feel an engine in my crotch that was like a rocket motor, the yellow fire starting to pour through gigantic expansion nozzles as it built up enough thrust for lift-off.

Her mouth opened wide but no sound came out. The long slabs of back muscle bunched tight and her spine arched up slowly, like a cat. Then I saw nothing more and dug my free hand into her hip, the other still entwined in her hair. The orgasm went off like a field of howitzers, the come as viscous and fiery as molten lava. The little electrical switches in my brain surged with extra voltage, snapping on and off and spewing sparks. I felt myself collapse atop her sweaty back and rolled with her to the floor.

The outside street noise came back slowly. I forced my breathing to go slower, even as my heart galloped. Vicki lay next to me, looking as if she'd just thrown herself across a marathon's finish line.

I looked at the ceiling and tried to make a pattern of the snaking watermarks. Couldn't. I closed my eyes.

Whenever had I come like this? Certainly not within recent memory. In college, perhaps? Hadn't there been some especially torrid night with a dark-haired girl I'd met at a poetry reading? The memory wisped by.

I hiked up on one elbow. Vicki's breathing had slowed, and, though flushed, she looked serenely peaceful. None the worse for wear, despite the hair yanking. I wondered if she had really been in pain. Vicki rolled into me, planting her face against my chest. I kissed the top of her head and brushed her hair tenderly. She hummed and nuzzled.

A gust of air slid across the sweat on my back, making me shiver. It was a beautiful day outside, but the warmth had gone out of it. Fall was on the way.

Ten

I didn't know how far I wanted to take this office romance. I didn't know if I wanted even one repeat performance. The more I looked at it, the more it seemed a bad mistake. Why had I let myself be taken to her apartment? I should have known what was going to happen.

Vicki, however, was ready for the next rendezvous. Whenever I walked across the bullpen she would flash a secret lover's smile, but I would only hurry on to my office, wondering if one of her co-workers had caught on. Which would be just what I needed. *Christ!*

It was coming up on the two-week anniversary of our one and only tryst when Vicki walked in and shut the door. Ed was out at one of the plants, chasing down a production problem. I wished I'd gone with him.

"I guess you want to talk."

"Is something wrong with me, Charles? Honestly, you act like I got herpes." She smiled at what I hoped was a stab at humor. "I thought for sure you'd have come over another couple times by now."

The swivel chair squeaked as I leaned back. I didn't know what to say. "Listen . . . it's not you."

She leaned on the desk and looked down at me, pert young breasts pressing at her blouse. "Why don't you drop by and we'll talk about it? How about later today?"

"Well, I'd love to, but . . ."

She pushed away and strode to the door. Just before she exited she threw me a look that made me feel like a gooey place on the sidewalk. This was followed by the loudest, most monstrous slam in the history of the eighteenth floor.

I threw my pencil on the desk and sighed. Shit. I had been half preparing for just such a showdown, absently marshaling all the reasons why we should never see each other again. One, that I was a married man. Two, such relationships were severely frowned upon by Aerotel. Three, there could by no stretch of the imagination be a happy ending. Four . . .

But that was all crap. The sound reasons had evaporated while Vicki was confronting me, and all that was left was the *real* reason, naked and unadorned. It wasn't being married that bothered me. It was the sex we had had. Or at least the perversity of it. I had gotten off so powerfully—and Vicki, too—simply because of the pain.

So . . . did that make me a sadist?

No way, I immediately told myself. No way at all. That hair yanking had been an accident. Or almost, anyway. And even if it wasn't, how did that stack up to the things described in *Juliette*? Like it was nothing, that's how. Call de Sade from the dead and he would classify it as an act of pristine innocence. Of course he would. He would laugh.

Or he might whisper in my ear, *Don't be such a coward, Charles. Find out who you really are. The only thing worth knowing is yourself.*

I let that thought dangle in the air, wondering where it had come from. I certainly hadn't puzzled it out. It had popped up whole and complete, as if uttered by a separate entity.

Find out who you really are. The only thing worth knowing is yourself.

I leaned forward, began drawing little circles on a yellow pad.

Who I really am . . .

Maybe that's what made Ruskin tick. Maybe that's why he seemed so satisfied, so content with life, so sure of his place.

And maybe that was why so many people went through life confused and unhappy. Because they refused to come to grips with their own selves. Or were *afraid* to. But Ruskin wasn't. He knew his own nature.

Which was . . . what?

I doodled on the pad, drawing nothing. I thought of *Juliette*. Now I wished I hadn't given it back. There was more to it than I thought. Surely there was.

I decided not to eat, but still left for lunch a good half-hour early. This would give me enough time to whip by the downtown library and pick up *Juliette*. I rolled down my sleeves and put on my jacket and stuck my head in my immediate superior's office and checked out. Mr. Anderson nodded, the bright fluorescents reflecting off his shiny bald spot, and he made some dry comment about my taking a lot of long lunches lately. I grinned as if he'd told me a joke. The guy was a monumental prick.

After ten minutes of stop-and-start traffic I arrived at my destination. There were a couple of bums standing outside, and one of them tried panhandling me. I brushed on by, but when I got inside the building I found the security manager and made a complaint.

I looked through the card catalog and found there were some critical essays and biographies of de Sade, but the only thing they had that he'd written himself was *Justine*, which was sort of a companion novel to *Juliette*.

I left, noting with some satisfaction that a cop was shaking down the bums. There was a parking ticket under the wiper blade. I took it out, tore it in half, let the pieces fall as I got in.

I drove a few blocks and lucked into a parking slot in front of B. Dalton's. A black-haired young woman dressed like a 1950s-style beatnik looked it up in a gigantic red book. Though she found *Justine* and *Philosophy in the Boudoir*, no luck on *Juliette*.

I walked across the street to what looked like a secondhand, hole-in-the-wall bookstore. But the storefront was an optical illusion, for there seemed to be more books inside than the entire Library of Congress. Each stack was jammed with paperbacks from the floor to the ceiling fifteen feet above. The aisles were so narrow two people couldn't get by.

This was the ticket.

But after much looking the only thing I found was *Justine*. I went to the cash register and spoke with a gnomelike little man who looked more like a pawnbroker than a bookseller. I told him what I was looking for and he reluctantly put down an ancient *National Geographic* and opened a thick reference book. He leafed through the pages and paused, then snapped it closed. He dragged over a fresh tome and went through that. Then another. Finally he got to something that made his eyebrows knit together. He began shaking his head sadly. "You can't get it, mister."

"Why not?"

"It's never been translated into English, that's why." He tapped the open page. "Only edition listed here is from 1903, a reprint from the original published in 1797. But it's in French. Can you read French?"

"I . . . no."

He sighed wearily. "I could get it for you, but there's not even a price listed. I'd have to write the publishers first, then call you when they wrote back. Course, the way it looks to me is like this is some kinda collector's item, so we're talking bucks. You'd have to leave a deposit."

"That's all right. Don't bother."

He hiked his shoulders and spread his hands. "Okay by me."

"Uh, are you *sure* it's only in French?"

"Sure I'm sure."

"But I . . ." I let the words trail off.

He looked a little irritated. "But you what?"

"Never mind. Thanks for your trouble."

"Yeah, yeah."

I went back into the sunlight, squinting against the brightness. Now you see it, now you don't. Welcome to "The Twilight Zone," Mr. Ripley. I forced a laugh, but it came out like a bark.

Someone touched my arm. "Charles."

I wheeled around and saw that it was Vicki Kimberly. "What're you doing here?"

She smiled winningly. "Fancy meeting you on the street."

"Have you been following me?"

A bright, false laugh. "Of course not, darling!" She closed the distance to six inches. Strong aroma of soap.

Darling?

She put her hand on my arm. "Listen, I feel real bad about the way I slammed your door this morning and all."

"S'okay." My eyes darted to the right and left, worried that an acquaintance might happen by.

"I just really want to talk, you know?" The pressure on my arm increased. "I just want to find out what's wrong."

"Nothing's wrong, for God's sake. Listen, why don't we get in the car?"

I went around and unlocked the passenger door of the RX-7. Brief glimpse of a perfect brown thigh as Vicki climbed in, slit skirt working to its designer's purpose. The door clunked closed and I went around and got in on my side. The rotary engine thrummed to life, and when I swung into traffic some fuckerhead nearly broadsided me.

We went to Vicki's place. By now it was one-thirty, deep into company time. She threw her purse onto the bean bag chair. She came to me lazily, draped one arm over my shoulder, and used her other hand to flick at one of my shirt buttons.

"Hey." It was almost a little-girl's voice. Coy-like. I cringed.

"Hello," I said stiffly. I made no move to embrace her.

Her eyes traveled up to mine. She regarded me in a timid, almost Bambi-like way. If this was to melt my hard old heart, she was barking up the wrong tree. I took her hand from my neck and undraped it, walked over to the windows.

"What is it?" I heard her call, a little bit of whininess creeping into her voice. "What is the *matter*?"

On the street below I saw two exotic young women walking hand-in-hand. What was the world coming to? I plopped into the bean bag chair and found myself sitting much lower than I had expected. Lord, what was I doing in this young girl's apartment? I felt ridiculous. Vicki sat next to me, or rather she knelt next to me (*that's right baby, beg*) and took my hand. "C'mon, Charley. Can't we at least talk about it?"

I hated people calling me Charley. "Vicki, my coming up here the other day was a big mistake."

"Listen, I don't care if you're married. Honest to God, it won't bother me if you can only see me now and then. I know you gotta spend most of your time with your family. But you can come and see me some times, at least."

"So I can drop by anytime and get my ashes hauled. Is that what you're saying?"

She looked pained, but she began massaging my hand in an intimate sort of way. "Well, I was kinda thinking maybe some-times we could go to the zoo or the park or something . . . you know, in between the times here. But if you only have enough time for that, I guess that's okay. Sure. If that's the way you want it . . ."

Now how could I respect a person like this? I found myself shaking my head slowly, like a banker turning down a loan.

"That was fantastic sex, Charley." It wasn't praise. It was a plea. "I never had it like that before, not with anybody. Wasn't it like that for you?"

I struggled out of the chair. Why had I ever let myself get involved with this slut? "There's no point to this, Vicki. I'm sorry it happened."

Her face twisted. "What *is* it with you? What kinda *creep* are you? I feel sorry for your *wife*."

I had my hand on the doorknob, but her last word made me freeze. "What?" I asked, very quietly.

Something in her eyes brightened. "So that gotcha, huh? Afraid I might call little wifey and spill the—"

I had no conscious thought of moving across the floor, only that I was somehow on top of Vicki, hands tight around her fragile throat.

The rage inside was like a live thing, an eagle that had suddenly taken wing. "Don't you *ever*! Don't you *dare*!" The words hissed through clenched teeth, barely intelligible.

The whore's eyes were wide with total surprise. She pushed against me but her hands had no strength. I watched her face, fascinated, and felt the rage change to something else.

I wanted to see her die. I wanted to experience the sensation of life slipping from her body. I wanted this more than anything in the world, and I did not care why or what it meant.

Her face began turning blue. Her eyes strained at their sockets.

Then I was off her, gasping at the strength of my unexpected orgasm. Vicki rolled on the floor, coughing.

When I got home I went straight for the Jacuzzi, as if I might find oblivion in its bubbling foam. I felt strangely queer, as if someone had been following me.

"Hard day, dear?" Shelly smiled as she slinked into the sizzling waters, a glass of wine in each hand. She wore a bathing suit I'd never seen before, one which showed to advantage the new flatness of belly.

I took the wine. "Just the usual bullshit." I sighed as I lay my head against the tub's wooden lip.

Shelly told me of her day, which was the usual round of loading up the dishwasher and visiting the fitness center. I had never thought she'd be content to putter around suburbia all day, but I guess I was wrong. So wrong.

"Well, since you're not listening I might as well get dinner started."

"What's that?"

Tiny bubbles sloshed off her as she stood. "I said it's time for me to get dinner started."

"Aw, c'mon." I took her hand and hoisted myself upright. "No need to run off when things were just getting off the ground."

She giggled, pique gone. "What things?"

I wrapped my arms around her and her eyebrows raised pleasantly. I cupped her ass, found it newly firm. God, where the hell had I been? I put my lips against her ear. "Is señora on vacation long? Perhaps your husband weel not be back for awhile . . ."

Shelly laughed and slithered from my grasp. She walked toward the house briskly, glancing back and smiling broadly. I stood there, dripping, hands cupped as if I were still fondling her. There was no hint that I had done something wrong, or that she was somehow angry.

I sat back down and finished off the wine, warm water sizzling around my armpits. The muscles slowly unknotted. Then I heard the far-off ringing of the phone; two rings before Shelly picked up the kitchen extension.

Hello, Mrs. Ripley? My name is Vicki Kimberly, and—

My guts tightened unpleasantly. I wondered how much trouble Vicki could cause.

Plenty, brother. More than plenty.

I let my mind drift back to Vicki's apartment. Every particle, every dust mote, every contraction and relaxation of her face were as clearly vivid as if shot on videotape. I had never known such an intense experience. Was it because I had nearly choked the life from the young girl? I looked at my hands and they seemed the claws of an alien creature.

What the hell was going on? Why was the world coming apart?

I looked over at the Marsh place. Ruskin stood beside the barbecue, tongs in one hand and a Coors in the other. He flipped over a good-sized steak and ran the coolness of the yellow can across his sweating brow.

He saw me and waved. I waved back.

I stayed up late, drinking and watching television.

Ruskin was a man who had his little flings, and yet I would have been surprised to learn that even one had backfired. Even that romp with Debbie Hartfellen had come out all right.

And I had the feeling his luck not only extended to love affairs, but to other things as well. Perhaps everything in his life worked to his own liking. But how? What was the secret?

When I could no longer follow what was on the television, I staggered into the bedroom, where Shelly was already in deep sleep. I climbed onto the waterbed and let my face fall to the pillow. The bed gently sloshed back and forth, and I felt as if I were in the soft hand of a giant. A benign giant that only wanted to take good and loving care of me.

As I fell asleep I had the vague impression of being in a corridor with many doors stretching before me endlessly. I pushed one open. Inside were Ruskin and Debbie Hartfellen, both nude, both on the floor. Ruskin turned to look at me. His eyes were giving off their own white radiance, actually glowing. He worked his lips once and I read the word "Charles."

Debbie did not turn to look at me. There was no way she could. Because, you see, she was dead.

But, I saw, still very much pliant.

And Ruskin was . . .

There was a scream. It was terrible, long and agonized. My nervous system snapped tight, making the hair on the back of my neck prickle.

The scream had not come from Ruskin. Nor had it come from me.

Ruskin raised his hand and beckoned.

The scream came again, and it was a man's scream, from faraway.

I clawed my way to wakefulness, the waterbed churning and sloshing. Shelly's fingers dug painfully into my arm. *"Charles! Charles! Wake up!"*

Eleven

I threw the covers aside and swung my feet to the soft carpeting. My eyes were as wide as half-dollars, straining in the darkness. My mind raced in nonsense circles, and I did not know for sure if I were awake or was still in the midst of dreaming.

Then the scream came again, making Shelly gasp. The scream was unmistakably real. It was happening.

"What is it?" she hissed. *"Jesus Christ on earth, what is it?"*

I opened the nightstand's drawer and withdrew my snub-nosed Colt .38. The inside of my chest was like a sack of ice. I padded into the hallway, clad only in boxer shorts. The scream came again, this time with less force, a warbling, terrible sound. I froze, trying to figure where it was coming from. Outside. Way outside. Shelly bumped into me.

"Charles—"

"Sssh!"

Nothing. No sound. We proceeded into the living room, Shelly knotting the belt of her floor-length robe. I went to the sliding glass door and pulled the drape aside. The tiny backyard was painted in grays and blacks. A quarter moon rode low in the sky. I unlatched the door and slid it open.

We stepped out together, the .38 extended like a talisman. I wasn't breathing. I don't think Shelly was, either. Slowly, quietly, we stepped up onto the Jacuzzi deck. It was utterly quiet—even the crickets had fallen silent.

The scream came again, and it was a bellow of pure agony. Much louder out here. Christ, much, much louder. Shelly slammed against me, hugging me tightly.

"The valley," I said. "It's coming from the valley."

"Oh, god."

Our valley. Someone was being killed in *our* valley.

Another scream—a tearing, hideous sound that floated up from the canyon and filled the night. Shelly buried her head in my chest. I thought of the Mexican that had been killed in the valley on the other side of Mesa Vista.

I grabbed Shelly by her shoulders and held her at arm's length. "Get in the house and call the police!"

"Charles—"

"Tell them it's an emergency! *Hurry!*"

I stepped off the Jacuzzi deck and headed toward the edge of the backyard.

"*Charles, where the hell do you think you're going!*"

I turned. "Someone's being killed down there! I've got to stop it!"

She came off the deck, hurrying toward me. "*No you don't! No you don't!*"

I went ahead anyway. But stopped when I came to the shrubbery that ringed the canyon's lip. I looked down. It was black as midnight in a coffin.

Shelly grabbed me. "No way you're going down there, Charles! No way! What if there's a bunch of them?"

I licked my lips. Indeed, what if there were a whole group of them?

The scream came again, shooting up out of the blackness. We tensed up, holding onto each other tightly.

"Maybe you're right," I whispered.

"C'mon, let's get back in the house."

We hurried back inside. I put the pistol down and punched 911 on the trimline. I told the dispatcher there was a murder being committed, told her as much as I could. I heard a beep in the background, meaning I was being recorded. She asked for my address. I gave it, hung up.

Shelly handed me my bathrobe and I belted it on.

"They coming?"

I nodded.

She hugged herself at the elbows. Her face was drawn. "What do you think it is, Charles? Another one of those illegal aliens?"

"Yeah, I'm af—"

Another scream hit our ears. We went into each other's arms.

"The cops will be here any minute," I said through clenched teeth. "Any minute. Any minute now."

Then the screams began to come in a series, one shriek after the other, building higher. Shelly began to cry. I let Shelly go and went into the kitchen to look at the big wall clock. It was quarter after two. The shrieks continued. I paced from the kitchen to the sliding glass door and back again. The seconds went by slowly. The lusty sound of the earlier screams gave way to something that was horribly pitiful. I went back to the Jacuzzi deck. Some lights had come on across the ridge, over at Viewscape Estates, and distantly I could see the shape of a robed man peering into the valley. The screams, lessening in volume, continued.

How ghastly could things get? I was scared. Scared and enraged at the same time. And helpless. The screams, though faded, continued. When oh when would the goddamn police arrive? I went back into the house and saw that Shelly was on her knees by the sofa, two of the big pillows jammed against her ears. *Where were the fucking police?* I thrust my hands against my ears and grimaced. Still I could hear the screaming—only now it was a ghastly, animal moaning, a sound of absolute, rock-bottom despair. *What a night! What a dreadful, horrible night!*

Then, faintly, the sound of approaching sirens. Relief flooded through me.

I ran to the front door. As I passed the kitchen, I saw that four minutes had passed since I placed the call. *Four minutes!* I grabbed the knob and swung the front door wide. I trotted down the walkway and stood at the curbing.

Two police cruisers squealed onto the street, their light bars a stuttering brilliance of red and blue explosions. I raised my arms and waved. Their sirens warbled down and off as they approached. The nose of the first cruiser dipped as the driver applied brakes, and the door swung open as the Dodge seesawed on its shocks. A beefy young cop quickly clambered out, slipping a nightstick into his utility belt's ring. His broad face was grim. He looked at me questioningly.

"Out back," I said, "Out back in the canyon—someone's screaming."

We trotted to my backyard, going between my house and the Marshes'. Our backs were bathed in red and blue light, our shadows oscillating before us. The cop's partner was close behind. I could hear the footfalls of the cops from the other cruiser. And distantly, the sound of another approaching siren.

We came to the lip of the canyon and saw a black silhouette struggling up out of the valley. The cop reached for his service revolver.

"*Ruskin!*" I shouted.

Blue light bathed his face, then red. His mouth was half open, and his forehead was covered in grime.

He looked at the cop and pointed down into the valley. "Down there," he barked. "There's three of them. They were working some guy over when they saw me, and then they started to run." Ruskin pointed south. "They took off that way."

"You say there's three?"

"Three plus the guy they left behind."

The cop took his partner by the shoulder. He was an even younger guy, and his face looked drawn and tense. "Get back to the cruiser," the cop said. "Get on the air and tell them what's going on. Call the paramedics. The helo's going to be overhead soon; get ahold of them and tell them the suspects are on a southerly route."

The partner ran back to the cars. The cop withdrew his pistol and, glancing wordlessly at the two policemen from the other cruiser, went down into the valley. The other cops unholstered their revolvers. One of them snapped on the beam of a powerful flashlight. They followed.

Ruskin watched them descend, rubbing the back of his hand across his lips. Their progress through the brush was noisy.

"Christ," I said softly, stepping near Ruskin. "You went *down* there?"

He nodded quickly, not looking at me. "When I heard the screaming, I called the police. They said they were already on to it. I . . . got restless waiting for the cops. That screaming, you know, it was awful." He looked at me, breathing hard. Red shone on his face, then blue. "I only got halfway down when those people saw me. They took right off."

"Did you see what they were doing?"

He shook his head. "Only that they had some guy on the

ground. I didn't go to him. As soon as those people took off, I came back up."

Someone came running from the street. It was the cop who'd gone back to make his radio call, and his flashlight bobbed as he approached. He rushed on by and down into the canyon.

Then we heard the chattering of a helicopter. We could see its lights off to the east. The chattering grew throatier, and I could feel its hammering vibrating in my chest. I turned to Ruskin to say something, but it was already too loud to talk. Ruskin was staring at the helicopter intently, hands in the back pockets of his jeans. The pocket's stitching identified them as Sergio Valentes. Ruskin's dark blue sweatshirt was rolled up to his elbows. The helicopter came in low, and when it was almost upon us a bright little searchlight came on and sliced down into the canyon. The beam swiveled to the right, then left. The tail of the helicopter swung around slowly, then steadied up when the aircraft's nose was pointing south. The shubbery at our feet began to shake and pull at its roots as a strong gust of wind buffeted us.

Helicopters have always made me uneasy. I saw one crash once, in the South China Sea, and a good friend of mine was aboard. That memory has always remained with me, and now it came back to me vividly. At least, I told myself that was why the pit of my belly felt full of lead. It had nothing to do with the dark clothes Ruskin was wearing ... or with his words, a chant that kept repeating itself in my mind: *Maybe they did it just for fun.* The helicopter began chuffing south, the narrow spotlight beam raking the valley.

The young cop came crashing up out of the canyon, the one who'd been sent back to the cruiser earlier. He reached us and began walking back to the street, but I put my hand on his arm and stopped him.

"What's going on?" I asked. "What happened down there?"

Red and blue light alternately bathed his drawn face. Sweat beaded his forehead. His eyes were on me, but they were looking at something else, something far away. "I just got out of the police academy last week," he said—stupidly, I thought. "This is my first—this is my first—"

Then his eyes rolled up and I thought he was going to faint. But he merely leaned forward and let go with a dark, abrupt stream of vomit. I stepped out of the way in the nick of time, shocked and repulsed. I looked at Ruskin helplessly.

Then quickly looked away.

I watched the cop heave out his guts, telling myself this was a sickening spectacle. A *horrible* spectacle. That was what made me see something that wasn't really there. I hadn't seen the grin on Ruskin's face. It was a trick of the red-blue light. I was too wrought up from the screams, from the helicopter, from the retching cop, from all the horrible events of this horrible night. I hadn't seen it at all.

Twelve

I rolled uneasily on the waterbed, unable to sleep. Shelly had managed to drop off only a few moments before. The glowing digits of the bedside clock said 4:00 A.M.

I closed my eyes, and was immediately granted an instant replay of the paramedics bringing the body up from the canyon. It was on a stretcher, and the sheet had been splotched with dark blood. I opened my eyes and sat up, sweat beading my forehead.

Ruskin had gone down there to help that man. Of course he had. What else could it have been?

I got out of bed and went to the kitchen. I turned on the Mr. Coffee and poured in water for six cups' worth. I twisted the dial on the breakfast counter's Sony and found an Abbott and Costello movie. The aroma of coffee began to fill the kitchen.

What else could it have been? My imagination was just overactive, that was all. Surely.

I poured the coffee, and after a moment's hesitation, slopped in a generous measure of supermarket-brand Scotch.

We went to a cookout one week later. The prime topic of conversation was the killing. The victim turned out to be yet another illegal alien. Some wondered out loud if property values might be affected. Police patrols were reported to have been stepped up from none at all to at least one cruise-through a night.

And there was darker speculation, whispered over icy cans of beer as the steaks sizzled. This had to do with the exact nature of the Mexican's death. I avoided these knots of people.

I overheard that the police hadn't caught any suspects, despite the assistance of the helicopter. And from somewhere in the back of my mind, something whispered, *Of course not.*

I found Shelly and we left before the first steak was ready. She kept asking what was the matter, but what could I say?

I drank a lot before I went to bed that night. But ended up bolting awake in the early hours with those same screams ringing in my ears, with my wide eyes looking into the blackness and seeing a toothsome grin hanging in the air, like that *Alice in Wonderland* drawing of the Cheshire Cat. Then I went to the kitchen, got a jug of wine, and sat down before the television and watched "CNN Headline News" until the alcohol did its job.

There was a party the next weekend, but I insisted we not go. I told Shelly I wasn't feeling well, but the truth was I knew I couldn't handle any of the cocktail conversations about the dead Mexican.

Shelly went ahead anyway, alone. It was over at the Coopers', three blocks away. Shelly came back early, looking a little dazed. There'd been an ugly incident, she murmured. *Two* ugly incidents, actually ... Burt Hartfellen had nearly killed Cal Baisley, who'd been idiot enough to make some crack about Burt's still-missing daughter. And the party didn't break up after the fight was over, as it once might have. People were getting used to this sort of thing, Shelly guessed. The party kept rolling right along, setting the stage for incident number two.

Dorothy Southwood, a mousy girl in her early twenties, had somehow wandered away from the Coopers' backyard. This was after Mesa Vista's new tradition of skinny-dipping had gotten well under way. Dorothy had wandered off unclothed. And dead drunk, of course. She staggered and sang her way across four blocks before an alert citizen noticed her and called the cops. The police found Dorothy on a dark stretch of Silas Street. She was in the backseat of a Road Runner, the co-owners of which were two tough-looking teenagers from God knew where, out for a cruise. The police broke it up while the junior of the two hoods was working on sloppy seconds.

My armpits felt wet and clammy while Shelly told me all this. I had met Rick Southwood once before, a mild and shy kind of guy who was a production engineer out at Rohr. And then—for just the barest instant—I thought I saw that Cheshire grin floating above Shelly's head. Only I wasn't dreaming this time, or waking up from one. *Or was I?* I thought crazily. I quickly got up and went to the kitchen, leaving Shelly in midsentence.

My hands trembled as I filled a tumbler with Mexican rum.

I felt a strong, atavistic unease, as if I could sense an impending earthquake. The glass clicked against my teeth so that I had to hold the the tumbler with both hands, and I raised it slowly as the sharp liquid splashed down my throat.

There was no sanctuary at work. I saw Vicki every day, and it increased my anxiety. We never spoke anymore, but occasionally our eyes would catch, and I would find myself looking into a hatred so strong and palatable it seemed to have a weightier texture than mere emotion. It hit me with an actual physical impact.

It was almost impossible to concentrate. Unwanted images kept drifting through my mind, images that were far more vivid and arresting than any mere daydream. A stick-figure person covered in flames. Vicki Kimberly blue and gasping as my thumbs pressed against her soft throat. A dark and silent canyon, biding its time until the void would once again be filled with screams that bespoke unbearable pain and complete hopelessness.

I had an awful feeling that some dark chaos was close at hand, pressing so hard against a once-sturdy door that the frame was starting to splinter even as the panels bowed in grotesquely.

"Oh, hello, Charles. Come on in."

Ruskin acted as if he'd been expecting me, even though I had decided to see him only moments before. I still had sawdust on my forearms from the halfhearted work I'd been doing on the bookcase. I followed him down the hallway.

"Guess the girls have gone off to their gym," he called over his shoulder.

"That seems to be their regular Saturday morning routine." My words sounded stiff and wooden, although, as I suspected I might, I was already beginning to feel a little better. Yes, as soon as I had crossed his threshold, I had begun to feel better.

He opened the door to his study and went inside. The shorts he wore were the same that he had so hastily doffed while entertaining Miss Hartfellen. Cool air gently hissed from an overhead vent, although it really wasn't hot enough outside to justify turning it on. He opened the little refrigerator and handed me a Michelob. I twisted off the cap. "Thanks."

"Woke up late today to an empty house," Ruskin said. "I thought Sybil had probably gone off with your wife. Have a seat."

The room had a more lived-in look. The rolltop desk was stacked with journals and notepads, and I wondered if I'd interrupted some paperwork. The little Ingram machine gun had been hung on a glossy mahogany mount. The miniature color television sat on a corner of the desk, sound turned off but picture bright with Saturday morning cartoons. I settled back into the chair comfortably, sipped my beer, and sighed.

Yes. Much better. I felt much, much better. Here was peace.

Ruskin sat in the fancy office-style chair and pulled out the writing slide. He opened the center drawer and withdrew a small round box.

"Care to get a little buzz on? You look like you need it, Charles. You seem a little peaked." He twisted open the box and with the practiced ease of a dentist arranging his tools neatly placed its contents on the writing slide. There was a small round mirror. A razor blade. A brightly colored child's straw, only two inches long. A small glass box about a quarter-full with what I believe the police call "a white, powdery substance."

I had heard that cocaine had migrated into the middle class, but never dreamt I would be in on it. But what the hell.

Ruskin arranged the powder into thin little rows, then graciously offered me the straw for the first . . . snort, I supposed. I leaned over the mirror and snucked it in, as I had seen done in news exposés on television. It stopped up my nose, but not so much that I couldn't reclaim the straw for my next turn. The lines disappeared quickly. Ruskin cleared off the writing slide, screwed the lid back on the box, and dropped it in its drawer.

My face felt as if it had been shot with Novocaine. My insides tingled and hummed, a sensation that was not unlike my brief experiences with speed back in college. It was nice. Very nice. Not only was my anxiety gone, but I felt a little rush of happy excitement. Of a sort of eagerness to get on with things.

Yes, coming over here had been the right thing to do.

I leaned back in the Barcalounger harder than I had planned and the footrest snapped up. I let my feet stay, the right foot quickly tapping back and forth.

Ruskin propped his feet on the desk and leaned back. He turned his tanned face to me and gave a smile fit for a travel poster. "Well, I feel a lot better now. Don't you?"

"Sure, great. Thanks."

"Sybil tells me you liked *Juliette*."

I smiled. I had been waiting for this. "Yeah. Matter of fact I'd like to get my own copy. Do you know where I can find one?"

He grinned slyly. "So far as I know, that book's only available in French."

"But how—"

"I got mine through a club."

"Book of the Month?"

"Not quite." He clasped his hands behind his head. "It's a club I belong to in San Francisco. Several years ago one of the founding club members translated it and had it privately published. Now it's one of the things each new member receives when they're accepted."

"Ah." So that explained it. Sort of. "What kind of club is it? A big, fancy gentlemen's club, like in England?"

He shook his head. "It's not like that at all. There are, for one thing, several female members. Sybil's one. And it's not in some big building with a smoking room and a game room." He paused and leaned forward, putting an elbow on the desk. "That's not exactly true, either. It *is* in a mansion, and there *is* a game room and a smoking room, but . . ."

"But not like a men's club in London."

"Yes, just so."

"What's it called?"

He looked at a stack of papers. The pause seemed overly long, as if he were thinking something over.

"The Society of Friends." He leaned forward and grinned at me. "Yes, that's what it's called." He laughed shortly, as if embarrassed. "I hope I'm not making it mysterious."

In some far corner of my mind a rusty relay turned over. "The Society of Friends . . . where have I heard that name before?"

"There's another group with the same name. It's the Quakers; they also call themselves the 'Society of Friends.' Like the 'Latter Day Saints' are Mormons."

"But there's no connection between you and the Shakers?"

"No, no connection. And it's Quaker, not Shaker. Quakers are different than Shakers. You know that guy with the big blue hat and long white hair on the Quaker Oats box? That's a Quaker."

"Uh-huh." My foot was still tapping rapidly. My cocaine-laden brain took the Quaker ball and ran. My only other knowledge of Quakers was a war movie called *The Deep Six*. In it Alan Ladd plays a Quaker naval officer. The dilemma is how he deals with the peace-loving dictates of his religion. Ends up hosing down a bunch of Japs with a burp gun. Or were they chinks? "Is this a secret club, like the Masons?"

"Well . . . I don't mind telling you about it, Charles."

"So, what do you do?"

"What do you mean?"

"What sort of club is it?"

Ruskin gave a minor shrug. "Like any kind of club, I guess. Just a group of people with common interests."

"Which is what? Sitting around reading de Sade?"

He looked at me and smiled patiently. "Charles, does that really strike you as incredible?" His tone was of the utmost reasonableness. "Don't you think it's worthwhile to broaden one's horizons?"

"Yes, but—"

"But what? Only in ways that would"—he gestured impatiently with his hand, searching for the word that would give voice to the contempt on his face—"suit a bunch of old women at a church social? What purpose would that serve? None, Charles. None save hypocrisy." He tapped his chest lightly. "Deep down, Charles. Where I live. That's what I care about, and wonder about, and an organization like the Society is dedicated to that sort of . . . learning."

"Exactly what sort?"

His eyes searched the ceiling as he groped for words. "It's hard to sum it up in one phrase, Charles . . . but let's call it self-knowledge."

Ruskin slowly brought his eyes down and looked at me steadily and surely and somehow . . . inquisitively. The air-conditioned breeze blew against my neck, making the hairs prickle.

"Self-knowledge . . ." I said slowly, not knowing what sentence I was beginning, and ultimately letting the word hang by itself, echoing in my mind as I pondered what it truly meant, and where it might lead.

To a dark canyon where an illegal alien might be happening by?

I thought of Vicki, of the way her eyes had bulged from their sockets as I pressed my thumbs against her windpipe, and the shocking force of an orgasm that had come out of nowhere, but had been far more powerful and sensual than any I had known before. . . .

The telephone buzzed. Ruskin picked up the cordless handset. "This is Mr. Marsh," he said in a quick, businesslike voice. "Uh-huh. Tell me about it, then. Uh-huh. Uh-huh. Yeah? And then what? Are you there now? All right, stay put and I'll be over in a minute. Yeah, sure, sure. Listen, call Sam and get him out there, too."

He recradled the phone and swiveled toward me. "Something's come up at the office."

I began to get up. Regretfully. "Well, I've got some things I should be doing myself."

"Oh, don't go just yet. I've still got plenty of time." He waved me back to my chair. He stood and opened the refrigerator, handed me a fresh beer. "Stay for a little while longer, Charles."

"No, really, I've got to be—"

He extended the frosted bottle and I took it. "You came over here to talk about something," he said soothingly, "and you haven't gotten to it. Tell me about it while I get dressed."

I twisted the cap and a tiny bit of foam oozed from the top. I nodded slowly. He was right; I *had* come over to talk about something, although I hadn't known it then. I found I very much wanted to talk about one specific thing.

I told Ruskin about Vicki Kimberly.

The words spilled out seemingly of their own accord, as if my brain wanted to excise the whole affair by a sort of verbal catharsis.

Ruskin shouldered into a light blue button-down shirt. "So she kept pestering you to come up to her apartment?"

"Yes, and I knew what would happen as soon as I consented to go. But I just couldn't stop myself, I—"

"Oh, don't torment yourself, Charles. Who can blame you?" He tucked the shirt inside his tan slacks. "You're not the first married man to be seduced by some young adventuress."

I nodded slowly. Lord, did it ever feel good to talk it out. The situation was coming into its proper perspective. "But it wasn't so simple as being seduced," I found myself saying. "If only it were something that . . . natural."

Ruskin was working a four-in-hand knot with his tie, but froze the operation in mid-loop. "What do you mean?"

"Well, the sex itself, Ruskin."

He smiled, but somehow it did not touch his eyes. "No healthy little romp in the hay?"

"No, far from it, Ruskin. She got off on . . . well, she got off on pain."

He swallowed thickly and finished with his tie. I told him how I had tried to end the affair, but that Vicki had kept following me and pleading for another rendezvous. Ruskin put on a beautifully tailored serge jacket and sat back in his chair. He looked at me levelly.

"Well, it's an old story, isn't it, Charles? But I think you're right to be concerned. You never know when one of these things might blow up in your face, especially when it involves someone at the office. That not only puts your home in jeopardy, but also your career."

I could only marvel that Ruskin had gotten so quickly to the meat. "Yes . . . yes, that's the way it is. But what do you think I should do?"

Ruskin picked up a pen and began to doodle on a large yellow legal pad, as if this helped him with his thinking. I took another sip of beer, finishing the bottle. His eyes flicked from me to the pad and back again. "I'll bet she's good-looking, right?"

"Huh? Oh, yeah. Real nice."

"Good body?"

"Real nice body."

"Big tits?"

I shrugged. "Medium."

"Face?"

"Good face, very cute."

He nodded slowly; fully dressed, he looked like any lawyer deep in consultation with his client. "What did you say her last name was?"

"Kimberly."

He wrote it down. "I suppose she's in the book."

"Book?"

"The phone book. I thought I'd give the young lady a call." He looked at me innocently, eyebrows raised. "Unless, of course, you're not really *sure* that you've finished with her."

"I don't understand."

"You want to get her off your hands, don't you? Let me have her. I'll take her mind off you."

"Let you have her how?"

He snorted with exasperation. "How do you think? Listen, she's just some office cunt out for a little fun, right?"

"Well, yes."

"A sweet young thing that wants to try a few married men before she settles down, right?"

"Yeah . . ."

"Well, I'm in the market for sweet young things right now. She wants to find out about grown men, I'll be happy to oblige."

"So what are you going to do? Just call her out of the blue?"

He was utterly confident. "Sure."

"What will you say?"

He turned his attention to the yellow pad, doodling with great force. "From what you've told me I think I've got her pegged. You say she likes it rough, eh?"

"That's right."

He chuckled lowly. "Believe me, I know *precisely* what to say. And by this time next week she probably won't even remember who you are." He glanced at his wristwatch. "Listen, I'm getting a little behind . . ."

I stood. "Sure, yeah. I gotta go myself." My mind worked at what had just happened. Could the problem be taken care of as simply as this? Would Ruskin really take her off my hands?

We walked down the hallway and out into the bright sunshine.

"I like doing coke on Saturday mornings," Ruskin said. "It makes you eager to get on with your work, rather than lazing the day away."

We both laughed as we shook hands, two youngish men on a bright morning in a prosperous development, taking their leave as one returned to his home hobby shop and the other to an emergency call from his office.

But as soon as I came off the cocaine high, I began to feel uneasy. What if Ruskin botched the call? I could see it now—Vicki tearfully and loudly accusing me of being a louse, with the whole eighteenth floor as witness. Oh, sweet Christ, I could see it.

But my fears proved to be groundless. I came in early Monday, and Vicki only gave me a cursory glance as I crossed to my office. No look of hatred. Indeed, she looked at me with absolutely no recognition at all.

I made it to my office and took off my jacket, took the top sheet from an overflowing In basket. Had Ruskin actually had the gall to do it?

Of course he had, I told myself. If any man did, it was he. I wondered what he had told her when he called her up.

I shook my head in admiration. You really had to hand it to that guy.

The week went swiftly, each passing day heaping confirmation upon confirmation that Vicki was no longer interested in me. Or even angry that I had palmed her off on another man. And the tempo of work increased dramatically due to an unexpected turn of events. Aerotel had hired a team of management specialists to look over the entire operation and make recommendations, we were told at a staff conference.

"That's all we need," Ed told me later. "A bunch of gunslingers out to chop off the deadwood."

There was much consternation and overtime. I spent many long hours at my desk, and only once or twice did Vicki Kimberly come into my view. And then it was only as another overworked drone, so busy with her secretarial chores she barely had time to let me sign the papers she shoved my way. I treated her with the same lack of recognition, as if our one intimacy had never occurred, and I hardly noticed the dark circles under her eyes, nor the gaunt cast to her face.

Then two things happened on the same morning.

For the third day in a row I noticed Vicki was not at her desk. As casually as I could manage I chatted with the head secretary, a white-haired old gal everyone called "the Iron Bitch." Yes, she said, Vicki was gone for good. This information was passed over her shoulder as she attended to some important filing. Vicki had gone back to Remington, Indiana, no longer intent upon seeking fame and fortune in California.

"Kind of abrupt," I said.

"Surely was, Mr. Ripley." She paused in her filing, brushing a white-haired lock from her forehead. "Usually they just leave after they collect their last paycheck, but Vicki was nice enough to write me a sweet little letter."

"Oh, really? What did she say?"

"Just the kind of stuff you'd expect from a young girl. How much she missed home and was looking forward to going back, how she was thinking of going to college, that sort of thing. Why do you ask?"

I found the strings that made my lips pull back in an affable grin. "Oh, nothing. Just wondering."

I went to my office, feeling as if I were making an awkward attempt to walk on stilts. I sat at my desk and looked at my calendar. Three weeks since Ruskin said he'd take her off my hands . . . Christ, what had he done to her? What had made her go back home? I thought of Debbie Hartfellen, who left town shortly after being screwed by Ruskin.

I sat back in my chair, patting a handkerchief at my upper lip. Whatever Ms. Kimberly decided to do wasn't my business anymore. And now that she was gone, there was absolutely no possibility of her calling my wife. Her book was safely closed. I should feel nothing but happy relief.

Still . . . there was no reason why a person shouldn't be interested in what happened to a former lover, was there? What would it hurt to call her home, just to make sure she made it back okay? Simple enough to look up the area code for Indiana, and then ask for Remington information and get the number of Vicki's parents. It was just the concern of an interested party that made me talk with a frail-sounding old lady, who wept that she hadn't received a card or letter from her daughter in a month, that Vicki's phone in her Hillcrest apartment was reported out of service. I listened to her plea for some information about her daughter, but as I recradled the phone I thought that some stones really were better left unturned, that one should let sleeping dogs lie, and that Aerotel was paying me to hack my In basket down to size instead of wasting valuable time.

Then, around ten o'clock, the other thing happened. Ed walked in the office, stiff-legged, eyes wide, face ashen. He wasn't hung over. I noticed his old-fashioned dispatch case had been next to his desk all morning; he had actually made it to work on time for once, only instead of being at his desk he had been . . . where? He made it to his chair and sat heavily. "Jesus, I've been fired."

"What?"

"I'm out. Gone. Shitcanned."

"You're kidding."

"Eighteen fucking years I've been here, and boom. Heave-ho." He opened his satchel and began stuffing it with his few personal items. One of which was a half-empty flask. He took a stiff knock, then offered it to me.

"No thanks, Ed."

He grinned lopsidedly. "What's the matter? Afraid you might catch the disease?" He took another swig. "Never know who's going to be next. Those fuckers are just getting started. Yes, sir. Just . . . getting . . . started."

The coffee in my stomach turned to acid. Trim-the-fat time at Aerotel.

Dear God, was there ever going to be any peace again? That feeling was back, that awful surety that an avalanche was about to start rumbling downhill, crushing everything in its path.

Thirteen

I passed the weekend uneasily. I tried working on the bookcase, but for some reason wound up slamming the power saw to the concrete floor, smashing it. *Cheap goddamn thing.* And I turned on the bookcase, giving it enough of a solid kick to make it collapse. *Stupid fucking hobby.*

I felt itchy and restless. Ruskin would make me feel better, I knew. He was the only person that would. His life had the serenity and peace that forever eluded me, and just talking to him made me feel I had stepped into the same tranquil pool, where everything was relaxed and made perfect sense.

But when I tried visiting him Sunday he wasn't there.

Monday there was a lean, rangy kid sitting at Ed's desk. His name was Jim, and the ink on his MIT diploma wasn't even dry. He greeted me brightly, called me "sir" with irritating frequency, and buckled down to work. Seemed like a punk.

I worked for a while but couldn't seem to get my mind in gear. I picked up the phone and called Ruskin at Techlydyne. As soon as he was on the line, I felt immeasurably better, as if he transmitted a certain kind of strength over the line ... a strength that succored me, whereas everyone and everything else were trying to drag me down.

I set up a lunch date at a place I was sure none of my co-workers frequented. Ruskin said he knew the restaurant, which surprised me. He certainly got around for a guy who'd been in town only a few months.

I headed out at twelve-thirty, not bothering to check out with that jerk-off Anderson. The restaurant was over in Mission Beach, about fifteen minutes away. I had been there once or twice a long time ago.

I drove out of the parking garage and took the nearest on-ramp to the freeway. Traffic was irritatingly slow. And when the Mazda finally found its way to the beach, I had to sweat out bumper-to-bumper traffic. There was no parking anywhere. I saw some old biddy in a battered Chrysler trying to parallel park unsuccessfully, so it was no problem for me to swing in the slot and take over. She honked her horn as I got out of the RX-7.

The Condor was a two-story bar and grill. I went inside and climbed the stairs to its open patio deck. I saw Ruskin right away—he stood out in his pin-striped lawyer clothes. I felt good as soon as I saw him, as if someone had pulled the switch on my anxiety. I walked over, waving hello. It was five till one.

"Hello, neighbor." His grin was exceedingly white against his tanned face. The sun glinted dully off his black aviator sunglasses. "The beach scene is a nice change for lunch. Good suggestion."

"Thought you'd like it." I pulled out the director's chair and sat on the blue canvas. God, I felt human again. "I used to come here a lot, a long time ago."

Ruskin nodded as he poured me a glass of wine from a large carafe. "San Diego certainly has a lot of different things to offer. Tony places up in La Jolla. Little coffee houses around the college campus. Western style steakhouses out in the desert. Mexican restaurants in Old Town." He looked around the Condor, smiling with vast approval. "And this. The party beach scene. Nice."

I sipped my wine, taking in the view. Standard dress for both men and women was short shorts and skimpy shirts, exposing a lot of carefully tanned hide. Hidden FM speakers thumped with rock. There were frequent explosions of laughter.

Even though it was October, it was warm as summer. The climatic condition known as Santa Ana was in effect, meaning the wind was coming in off the desert instead of the Pacific. Otherwise it would have been a little cooler, but not much. I felt a little uncomfortable in my suit, but it was only because of the heat. No one looked at us askance for being in our corporate uniforms. San Diego was the sort of town where everybody minded their own business.

I flipped open the menu. There were twenty different kinds of "gourmet" hamburgers, ranging from El Mexicano (salsa sauce, extra onions) to Waikiki (two slices of pineapple). The whole wheat buns were baked on the premises daily, according to a dainty calligraphic slogan.

A ripely endowed waitress appeared and asked for our orders. She wore a T-shirt with the Condor's logo, and bright red jogging shorts.

"I'll have a San Diegan," Ruskin said, naming the one that featured sprouts and avocado slices. "Well done, please."

I ordered the same. The waitress's brow furrowed as she wrote the orders, and I saw that close up her crow's feet were quite evident. Ruskin refilled our wineglasses. "So, what's up?"

"Nothing much, just thought it'd be nice to get together for lunch." But why the fib? Why couldn't I just come out and say . . . that I wanted to know what made him so serene when all else was turmoil? And share in that knowledge?

"Did you ever get together with Vicki?" I asked.

He shrugged. "We got it on a couple of times. It was okay."

"I've heard she's gone back home."

"Gone?" He shook his head and chuckled at some memory. "Strange. She was really into it."

"Yeah?"

"Oh, yes indeed." He looked smooth and slick, like a fashion model in *Gentlemen's Quarterly*. "A little hesitant at first, but that was only an act. I'm sure you found her the same." He sighed expansively, lifting his shoulders a quarter-inch. "But that little fishy's gone back to the sea. Too bad. I guess she was really a non-hacker after all."

He regarded me patiently, the pounding FM rock filling the silence.

"Ruskin, are you a sadist?"

He continued to smile, totally unsurprised by my question. "Depends on what you mean."

"Okay. Tell me what gives you pleasure."

He hesitated, lightly touching the tablecloth with his fingertips. I imagined him doing the same thing in court, fingers skimming along the bar of a jury box as he prepared to make a fine point. "I think it's important to know oneself, Charles. Maybe it's the only thing really worth knowing." His black sunglasses regarded me levelly. "Knowing what you'd do under any given circumstance. Knowing what sort of person you really are. Knowing the sort of things you're capable of."

"Like what?"

He spread his hands. "Like knowing whether you'd chicken out under fire. That's not an uncommon question men pose to themselves. How many have wondered about that? Haven't you? Well, I've been in combat and I know I'm not yellow. That gives me great satisfaction."

"Yes, but that's a good thing. What about a bad thing?"

A smile. "Charles, I expect you've seen enough of the world to know that at least part of human nature is to be cruel and mean, and for no good reason."

I nodded slowly. "But does that mean you should explore that behavior? Actually do something bad just for the sake of doing it? Just to see what the sensation is?"

"The important thing is not the act, but the way it affects your self-perception. Knowing who you really are, and of what you're truly capable."

He looked at me intently, the sounds of the restaurant loud but far from intrusive. I thought of the time he'd come up from the canyon, and my lungs felt like a cold, empty vacuum. I was scared. I was excited. But most of all, curious. Intensely curious.

"And if you followed all of your instincts, Ruskin, where do you think it'd eventually lead to?"

He sipped his wine thoughtfully. "What do you think?"

"De Sade says it's . . . killing people. Murder for the sake of murder."

He frowned slightly. "Then I take it you haven't finished the book."

I think my mouth hung open. "But what could be worse?"

He opened his mouth to say something but the words came out so softly that they were snapped up by the surrounding noise. I leaned forward eagerly, nodding as if I could hear.

Then reality seemed to slip a notch, as if I were on a staircase whose rotted treads were slowly giving way. The restaurant sounds faded to a low, constant roar, as if a seashell had been placed against my ear. Ruskin's big black Bausch & Lombs filled the universe: two black pools of obsidian spangled with two crystalline suns. And behind those glasses, I thought, the eyes might be devoid of pupil or iris, but all-seeing nonetheless. . . .

A group at the next table roared at a joke. An old Volkswagen clattered along the street down below, inordinately loud. The sun bathed each corner of the Condor's upper deck with intense brilliance. A soft, singsong voice hit my ears like some sweet, melodious chant, then the syllables made sense. The voice said, "Ruskin? Ruskin?"

We both looked up, somehow disoriented from the . . . trance? Standing next to us was a lovely young woman, an expression of tense anxiety on her face. "Ruskin?"

He stood. "Angela . . ." His lips were compressed into the thin lines of annoyance. "What're you doing here?"

"Why haven't you called, Ruskin? I waited all last night—"

He grabbed her arm and I could see the fingers dig in. "Quiet, girl." He turned to me. "Angela, I'd like you to meet my friend Charles Ripley. Charles, this is Angela Linsome."

I got halfway out of my chair and took her hand. "Angela Lindsay," she said to me, quietly. "Hello."

Ruskin's lips moved, but I could see his white teeth clenched together. "Won't you join us?"

Ruskin pulled out her chair and she sat silently. Ruskin seemed angry over the surprise visit from his . . . what? Yet another girl-friend? Whatever, her presence made me mad, too. Meaningful conversation between Ruskin and I was over for the time being. I looked at her angrily, but found it hard to sustain this feeling for very long because of her . . . well, it had to be admitted she was spectacularly lovely. She had a long, finely made face, with flowing hair so blond it was almost devoid of color. Her purple tank top revealed a full and lovely bosom, braless. She wore a long white skirt, cinched tight around her narrow waist. Early twenties.

Ruskin signaled for the waitress. "Have you had lunch, Angela?"

She shook her head.

"Well, then. You're in for a treat. These are the best hamburgers in town."

She looked up. "Oh, I can't. I'm a vegetarian."

His iciness melted a little. He put his hand on the back of her chair, focusing himself on her. His grin shone like pearls. "A vegetarian, eh? That's interesting. Can't bear the consumption of flesh?"

She said nothing. The waitress arrived. "Do you have a chef's salad?" Ruskin asked. The waitress nodded. "Good. A chef's salad for the young lady, and please, no strips of ham or anything. All right?" The waitress repeated the order, eyebrows knitted in concentration. "And would you also bring another glass? And another carafe? Thanks."

Angela kept her eyes on the table. It was obvious she wanted to be alone with Ruskin, and had this been the 1940s I might have excused myself. But women's lib was firmly in place, so I was free to think of her in terms of what she really was—a rude person who deserved no discreet courtesies.

Besides, I hadn't eaten.

I admired her beauty coolly. Even though she looked contrite and confused, there was a certain proud bearing that managed to show through. It would not surprise me to learn she was a lifeguard. Very self-possessed, self-assured. Except for now, of course, with Ruskin grinning at her like a shark.

He asked her what she had been doing this day, what happenstance had brought her to the Condor. Ruskin's mood was getting better, as if he'd decided Angela's arrival was a pleasant turn of events. Angela answered so quietly I could barely hear. She seemed uncomfortable. Ruskin was enjoying himself.

The meal arrived, set down before us hurriedly. I ate leisurely, determined not to leave until I was good and ready.

Angela sifted through the salad, checking for meat, I suppose. Ruskin nodded at the salad, chewing vigorously, and when he swallowed, said, "What about those eggs?"

Angela looked up. "Huh?"

"Those eggs." The salad was adorned with several slices of hard-boiled egg. "Isn't that meat?"

"Well, no. Not really."

"Uh-huh. What exactly is your hierarchy, then?"

"Hierarchy?"

"I mean, you're eating eggs, which is a kind of meat. Do you eat fish?"

"Well, yes. I do."

"All right." Ruskin smiled, warming to his theme. "You eat fish and eggs, yet you call yourself a vegetarian—"

"But I don't eat meat," she interrupted.

"Cow's meat, you mean."

She played with her salad. "That's right. No cows. No pigs. None of the higher animals."

"Why? Just because they have bigger brains? What if plants have feelings? Some people say they do."

She considered his question, a few loose strands of fine hair blowing across her forehead.

"But you've got to eat something," she said at last. "I guess if plants have feelings . . ."

"Then it's too bad for them?"

"Not like that. I mean, it would be like that hierarchy you were talking about. Plants would be at the bottom, fish in the middle, animals at the top." She looked at the chef's salad. "I'm not hungry anymore."

We talked for a little while longer. Angela once again drifted out of the conversation. She was distracted, obviously anxious for me to leave so she could have her talk with Ruskin. I finished my burger and decided I did not want dessert, even though it was included.

"Listen, I've got to get back to the office." I saw Angela's face light up with happy relief.

"Oh, before I forget," Ruskin said, "Sybil and I are having a party this Saturday and we'd like you to come."

"Fine. Say, isn't that—"

"Halloween? Indeed it is. It's a costume party, Charles. Sybil and I threw one every year in San Francisco, and we'd like to keep the tradition going down here."

Angela interjected brightly, "A costume party! What a fantastic idea!"

Ruskin and I swiveled our heads, surprised. I think we had both forgotten her presence.

"Angela, honey, this party is at my *home*." Ruskin's tone was soft and patient, as if instructing an awkward child. "That's where my *family* lives. You couldn't expect an invitation to my home, now could you?"

She looked down, cheeks blushing crimson. "No," she said quietly, "I guess not."

Ruskin turned to me, chuckling good-naturedly at her foible. But I kept my eyes on her, watching the tiny little tears slip from her tightly closed eyes. *Tears!* I shook my head in disgust. I'd had enough of young girls throwing themselves at married men. They deserved whatever they got. I felt nothing but contempt.

I stood and Ruskin came around the table and took my hand warmly. "Listen, sorry we didn't get a chance to really talk. I think we have a lot to talk about, you and I." The pressure on my hand increased. "I think we can be good friends."

"I'll be looking forward to this Saturday, then."

I weaved through the crowd and Ruskin returned to his lunch.

He needn't have told me about the party.

When I got home Shelly and Sybil Marsh were standing in the driveway and talking about costumes. I joined them, smiling at Sybil's clinging bodysuit—this one bright aqua. They said hello and returned to the thickets of their conversation. I went on inside.

Shelly put a great deal of thought into what she was going to wear. She and a few friends made more than one trip to costume stores—there were quite a few in San Diego, evidently filling a growing demand from aging baby-boomers unwilling to let go of Halloween fun. Shelly's outfit turned out to be a good copy of the one Princess Leia wore in *Star Wars*. I stopped by a costume store on the way home from work Thursday, and rented a cape and bought some makeup. I was going as a vampire.

Saturday rolled around and Shelly helped with my makeup—white face, dark circles under my eyes. I put in some plastic fangs, donned my cape, and was set. Shelly spent a great deal of time rolling her hair into those little buns on either side of her head. We walked over to the Marshes around eight.

Ruskin greeted us at the door, decked out in a scarlet riding jacket and top hat—circus ringmaster. Sybil was quite alluring in her Vampirella outfit, face whitened but not so much as mine, a deep, diving décolletage revealing the firm half-moons of her bosom. We went into the living room and saw they had hired a bartender for the night.

As soon as we had our drinks Ruskin was at my side, slowly ushering me outdoors. The Jacuzzi sizzled and bubbled like a witch's cauldron. We went into the darkness and he produced a marijuana cigarette. "Wait'll you try this." He grinned. "Absolute top-grade stuff from Hawaii. Maui Zowie."

He lit it and we passed it back and forth. It was indeed quite good, and I felt myself getting high rapidly. We were facing his house, the sliding glass doors revealing the room where he had put it to Debbie Hartfellen. Only now it was filling up with people, all dressed in wildly differing costumes. Laughter floated to our ears, and the thumping, repetitive sound of some old disco music. We smoked the bomber down, and Ruskin ground it out beneath his black riding boot. "Time for me to greet the rest of my guests."

We began walking back toward the house, my vampire cape trailing behind. I felt as if I were walking through warm oatmeal, heavy and pleasant and very high. "Where's Mark?"

"They're having a Halloween party of their own, over at the Simpsons. I believe they're watching videodiscs of old horror movies."

"And probably smoking shit like this."

We both laughed as we headed into the warmth and noise and light. Ruskin disappeared with the suddenness of a magician's trick. Or so it seemed to my dope-soddened brain. I pasted on a warm, friendly smile and began to mix.

I saw Sarah Weinburner in a corner, dressed up in a fetching little slave girl outfit, complete with satiny, billowy pantaloons. She was batting her eyes at a man who wore a green fright mask; he was leaning against the wall next to her, talking quietly. Shelly's grapevine had it that Ralph was living on the other side of town. I remembered her in the Hartfellens' kitchen, making out with some guy. Then the other, more turgid memory of her in the Jacuzzi with Ruskin, langorously beating him off. I became suddenly and powerfully horny, and began to lay my plans to get the trollop out back where there was some privacy. Maybe in the Jacuzzi, even. I smiled so that my plastic fangs showed.

God, I felt good.

I began working my way through the crowd, heading toward Sarah. Prying her loose from her monster was going to take some doing.

Then there was a hand on my arm, pulling me aside. It was someone dressed up like a monk, hood drawn down so I couldn't see the face. We went into the entrance hall, where it was relatively quiet.

The hood came back and I saw it was Angela Lindsay. "You're Mr. Ripley, aren't you? The guy who was with Ruskin the other day?"

"That's right ..." My horniness vanished instantly. I was stunned. "Did Ruskin invite you here?"

She bit her lip, looking down at the floor. "No, he doesn't know anything about this. I'm sure he'll be angry when he finds out."

"I'll say! This is his *house*, for Christ's sake. You know his *wife's* here?"

She looked over my shoulder, at the noisy crowd, then into my eyes. "I've got to see him. I tried to talk to him the other day when you left, but somehow ... well, we ended up not doing much talking the rest of that afternoon."

"What is it that's so important?"

She worked her hands nervously. Her eyes were wide, trying to figure out if I were someone she could trust. In that loose getup, which hid her voluptuous figure so well, she looked all of fourteen. "I—I'm pregnant."

I could think of nothing to say. I took a swig of my drink. I remembered that when Ruskin had introduced her he hadn't gotten her name right. "How far along are you?"

"A month and a half."

"Can't you get an abortion? I mean, isn't it easy?"

Again she put her hand on my arm. "I want to have it. I don't want to kill it. I really want it."

"Listen, I don't think Ruskin will divorce—"

"I know! I know! And it's all right. I won't ruin his marriage. But I've still got to tell him, don't I?"

I shook my head, not knowing what to think. Stupid, stupid girl!

She dug her hands in my arm. "Don't I? Don't I?"

"Yes, yeah, sure. But coming to his house isn't the right way to do it. Don't you see that?"

She let my arm go and looked into the crowd. "Somehow it seems he and I never really talk. And it's all I wanted to do ever since we first met. Just sit down and talk. But there never seems to be any time." She looked at me. "You're his friend, aren't you? You've known him a long time, haven't you?"

"Well, he just moved in."

"He talks about you a lot."

"*What?*"

And without further comment, she pulled up the hood and went into the crowd. I was apparently of no more use to her. I went over to the bar and had the bartender give me a double bourbon with a couple of ice cubes to help wash it down. I tossed it off and had him make another, then took this out back to drink it where there was some fresh air. I wanted to forget about little Miss Angela. I wanted to be high again, the way I was a short while ago with Ruskin. I wanted to pick up the threads of the conversation we had started at the Condor. That was the important thing.

I headed back toward the drinks, intending to see if the pimply bartender could handle a Black Russian.

Then another arm was slipped into mine. It was Sybil Marsh.

"Well, hello there, sexy lady."

"Charles, where have you been? I've been looking for you all evening." She drew me away from the bar, away from the sounds of the party. "I've been meaning to talk to you."

I smiled down at her. "Really, now?"

She pulled closer to me, pressing the warmth of her bosom against my arm. "You don't seem very happy tonight. What's bothering you?"

I held up my Black Russian. "Not high enough."

"Then come into my web, said the spider to the fly."

We were in another part of the house. Sybil opened the door to a bathroom and we went inside. She flicked on the lights and a small overhead fan began to whirr. "My bathroom. Ruskin's is on the other side of the bedroom." She opened the medicine cabinet and withdrew a small round box, finely made. Similar to Ruskin's cocaine box, but not the same one. His and hers coke boxes? I smiled warmly.

On the underside of the lid was a mirror, and she laid this across the tile counter. She took some white powder out of the box, placed it on the mirror, began forming it into little straight lines with a razor.

She looked up at me and smiled. Her breasts were nearly falling out of her Vampirella outfit. "Can't have one of my guests being all unhappy, now can I?"

"Guess not."

She took a little straw and put one end in her nostril and the other against one of the lines. Up it went, neat as a vacuum cleaner. She did another line, then stood, sighing with pleasure. She handed the straw to me.

I bent over and snorted. It tickled as it hit my nose hairs. I did another line and handed back the straw.

We took turns, doing all that was on the mirror. My nose was deadened, and the feeling was beginning to radiate over my face. I was high again, and it was a much better high than the first time I had used cocaine with Ruskin. Much better. The evening stretched before me endlessly.

Sybil looked at me coyly. "That do the trick?"

"Yes, indeed. I consider this very neighborly of you."

We laughed softly.

"Well, then," she said, moving very close to me. "Now that I've done you a favor . . ."

"Yes?" My heart began to race.

"Now it's time for you to do something for me."

I thought she was moving to put her arms around me, but her hands were on my belt buckle, pulling it loose. I put my hands on her shoulders to draw her near, but she slipped to her knees, pulling down my pants. My half-erect member wobbled free and was soon engulfed with a delicious, sweet warmth. I opened my mouth to sigh but no sound came out. Sensation compounded upon sensation until I felt on the verge of crying out. I couldn't breathe, yet would have been glad if I never took another breath. I buried my hands in the soft straw of her hair.

Ah, this was heaven, this was bliss. What did it matter that she was Ruskin's wife? He would understand. He more than any other. Was he not the one who had no use for the conventions of society? Was he not the one who had shown me that a man can make his own rules, based on the reasoning of his own sensibilities? You could submit to the nonsensical conventions of society, and go mad—or you could stand on your own two feet. What was it that Juliette had called those conventions? "Prejudice and superstition." But her Reason had won out. Yes indeed. Sweet Reason. I was untroubled now, and free.

The things that had bothered me would worry me no longer. They were the empty Halloween masks of children, carried off in an October wind. What counted was coming to know who you truly were. That's what gave life its meaning. That's what it meant to be alive. Freedom to chart your own course, and to stand alone.

Sybil stood, wiping her mouth. Slowly, lethargically, I pulled up my pants and zippered my fly. The whirring of the little ceiling fan seemed very loud. She turned to the mirror and brushed her hair, humming.

We went back to the living room, and Sybil melted into the crowd. It was very rowdy now. Some kind of game was going on, something like pin the tail on the donkey. Only the donkey was a life-size picture of a nude woman, and the tail was a pair of big plastic breasts with suction cups. I watched John Driscoll stagger toward the picture, blindfolded and drunk, plastic boobs extended straight out. He bumped into the picture and pressed the phony hooters against the midsection. Screams of laughter. I went over to the bar and got a beer, went outside and popped the top.

I felt wonderful. I felt as if I had gotten over a once-insurmountable hurdle, and was now suffused with a sublime victory. I was, at last, back on the path I had started in college. My mind was once again opening like a flower, as if gentle sunlight had drawn the petals wide to reveal the astonishing beauty within. And never again would anything stand in my way. I was on the threshold of a new phase of life, one that was full to over-flowing with wildly exotic wonders.

I looked back at the house. Ruskin was easy to spot in his bright red jacket. George Reed was now given the plastic breasts, and he giggled nervously as the blindfold was tied on. George was a fairly new guy in Mesa Vista, an instrumentation engineer out at Lockheed. He was short and fat, and very eager to be accepted by his new neighbors. He began staggering toward the nudie picture, wobbling like a child just learning to walk. Then Ruskin thrust out a black riding boot and caught George's ankle. Fat Boy went down abruptly, arms splayed wide. The house seemed to shake with the thunderous laughter. I myself was so convulsed I had to bow slightly over, holding on to my sides. I saw George push up on his hands, blindfold askew, looking around with an expression of confused embarrassment. My sides positively ached, and tears of mirth squeezed from my eyes.

Fourteen

I slept late the next day.

I got off the sofa and headed toward the bathroom, head throbbing unpleasantly. I stopped and looked back. Sofa? How had I wound up there? Tried to remember. Couldn't.

I hit the light switch and the bathroom's little ceiling fan began to whirr. The memories of last night flooded back. Or at least the early parts of it. It seemed murkily unreal.

I relieved myself, then brushed my teeth. Some of the Dracula makeup was still on, all smeared. My eyes were bloodshot slits. Needed a shave, but I would get to that later. I trudged into the bedroom, scratching my unkempt hair, feeling perfectly awful.

Shelly had one of her huge suitcases on the bed, into which she was industriously throwing clothes.

"What the hell's going on?"

No pause. "I'm going away for a few days."

"What?"

"You heard me, Charles." She went into her closet and got another armload. I intercepted her halfway back to the suitcase, grabbing her arm. Anger glowed dully, like a coal about to catch.

"Will you stop that goddamn packing and look me in the eyes!"

She did. "Take your hand off my arm, please."

I loosened my fingers. The tone of her voice was cold and dead, and it made me feel sick. "Did ... Sybil talk to you last night?"

She opened another drawer and lifted out a batch of underclothes. "Yes, she mentioned something." She flashed her eyes at me. "Something of great insignificance."

I sat heavily on the bed, right by the suitcase. "About what happened in her bathroom?"

"Yes," she said wearily, tossing in the clothes.

I bowed my head. It wasn't fair. Some guy like Ruskin runs

wild all he wants, and then a jerk like me strays just the tiniest, littlest bit . . . and bam, it blows sky high. "Shelly, darling . . ." I shook my head helplessly. "Christ, honey, I'm sorry."

She pulled the suitcase lid closed and snicked the latches. "That's all right, Charles. Things like this happen in the best of marriages."

I looked up, surprised. "What?"

"You heard me." She lifted the suitcase off the bed. "All's forgiven on that score."

I stood, palms outstretched. "Then why are you leaving? I don't get it."

This time it was she who bowed her head; it was her whose shoulders slumped. "This has been a long time coming, Charles. I don't think I love you anymore, and I don't think you love me."

"But, darling . . ."

She lifted her head. "Something's been wrong between us for a long time. We don't talk much anymore. We want different things out of life, I think. I'm not the same person I was when we got married, and I know you're not the same."

I put my hand on her arm, very softly. "Darling, all that means is . . . we're getting older, I guess. But it's nothing to leave me for. We can work it out. We'll talk. Stay, please."

She shook her head sadly. "If only it were that simple, maybe I would. But it's not."

"What's not?"

I could see it was costing her a great deal to look me in the eyes. But she kept the gaze steady. "Charles . . . I think I'm gay."

I opened my mouth to say something but nothing came out. My jaw hung stupidly wide.

Shelly moved away and got her shoulder bag. "Kick in the head, isn't it?" She slung the strap over her shoulder. "But I don't know how to make the truth prettier than it is."

My jaw began to work. "Wh—who?"

"Sybil. It's been going on for some time now." She put her hand on the doorknob. "And Charles, darling, don't think of it as your fault."

Three quick strides and I was at her side, fingers digging into her arm. "What the hell's gotten into you? Is she better than me?"

"*Yes! Yes! She's much better than you ever were!*"

The anger rose up so quickly and so completely that when I yanked her away from the door she actually lifted off the floor. I heard her gasp, and then she was tumbling on the carpet, shoulder bag and suitcase flying. She thumped up against the foot of the waterbed, half-upright, strands of hair hanging loosely over her face. And when she looked at me, I saw the expression did not so much convey pain as it did total astonishment.

"Charles?" Her voice was a little girl's whisper. "Charles?"

Bitch, I thought. Stupid goddamn *cunt*.

"*Charles!*"

I was almost upon her when she pushed herself up and began scrabbling across the waterbed on all fours, trying to get away. I lunged at her and almost caught her ankles, but she was too quick. I pawed after her, the waterbed churning and sloshing so violently it seemed like one of those nightmares where you try to run but your legs seem swallowed up in a vat of glue.

And nightmare it was, chasing the wife I had never struck before with this sudden, terrible urge to strike her many times. But I was trapped inside a mechanical body, and a stranger was at the controls.

Shelly swung her legs to the floor too quickly and so sprawled out of control. She knocked the nightstand over and the adjustable lamp swung crazily and the lightbulb went off with a small explosion. I pushed myself off the bed and rushed to her, got a firm grip on her arm before she could get away. I fully intended to slap her, but somehow found that my hands had locked to her throat and . . . and . . . It became something different, the texture changed, and I was filled with an emotion that I could not name. But it was something with which I was not entirely unacquainted. My hands pressed and squeezed, and I knew that this was no longer a mere husband-and-wife quarrel. Oh no.

It was a warm, viscous thing that flowed thickly and sweetly into my limbs and made me feel impossibly huge. I closed my eyes as the tumescence began. I felt on the verge of some great knowing, and I tightened my grip in the fear that if I let go I might swoon. The sound of her gasping and the flailing of her hands became distant and faraway.

Pain was a white-hot bolt, rocketing up out of nowhere. I cupped my hands to my groin and tried to cry out, but there seemed to be no breath in my lungs.

The pain held me tightly in its mighty grip, and the only thing I could do was roll helplessly on the carpet. Shelly coughed and gasped, the sound tiny and faint.

The pain grew more intense, making sweat pop out on my forehead. I clenched my teeth and closed my eyes tight and brought my knees up to my chest. I felt like I'd been castrated with a dull knife.

I don't know how long I laid on the carpet. I lost count of the long, slow radiations of unendurable pain, throbbing and washing over me in big greasy waves. But by the time the cadence seemed to be lessening I heard the sound of the Valiant starting up, and a clunk of gears as it backed down the driveway.

I carefully pushed myself from the floor; but when I tried to straighten my back the pain surged up afresh. I caught my breath and hobbled from the room, made my way to the kitchen.

I splashed cold water on my face and that seemed to help.

I opened the refrigerator and carefully poured myself a glass of orange juice. I drank it slowly. I washed my face again.

I made my way to the laundry room, still bent over, and looked out the window to confirm that the Valiant was indeed gone. I went back to the kitchen and poured another glass of orange juice, and, after a moment's hesitation, sloshed in some supermarket-brand vodka.

I eased myself into the chair in the breakfast nook, screwdriver ingredients handy. The pain had localized itself to the crotch area. I sipped the drink, mulling over the morning's activities.

After a while I dispensed with the orange juice.

When I woke up I found myself on the waterbed, with no recollection of how I'd gotten there. I sat up abruptly, telling myself that I'd just had a terrible dream. But when I saw the nightstand sideways on the floor, I knew that what had happened had been as real as real could be.

I got out of bed and had no trouble standing up. My groin was still tender, but the only real pain was a juicy little headache just behind my eyes. I padded to the kitchen and drank two tall glasses of spring water. Then I found a bottle of aspirin and washed down three tablets.

I stood there and stared out the window, looking at the soft light of late afternoon. Wondering when the enormity of what I had done would hit me.

But nothing came. I felt only the inner workings of my own body, the various organs and systems busy with their little errands. There was even a faint rumbling of hunger.

No, I didn't feel sorry at all. I could put on an act, of course. I could go chasing after Shelly and beg forgiveness. That would be what I was *supposed* to do . . .

Dimly, slowly, a memory tried to make itself known. Hadn't there been something last night about freedom, about charting my own course? Hadn't there been a moment of supreme contentment? Something about standing on my own, alone?

Let's try it on for size. Let's look at the situation without any adornments. I had nearly killed Shelly. I had actually been on top of her with my hands around her throat. And as I had tightened my grip, I knew that I was not angry over her infidelity, nor even over her leaving me.

So what *had* I been intent upon?

(*fun?*)

The phone rang. I looked at the kitchen extension, feeling no urge to pick it up. I wondered who it might be, if there were anyone I'd like to talk to.

Yes, of course. There was one.

The phone continued ringing, and I walked toward it without hurry, playing a childish game. If it was who I wanted, I would live forever. I would have riches without end. I would never grow old. I picked it up and said hello.

"Charles? This is Ruskin."

Warmth and relief flooded through me. "Hello, neighbor."

"Listen, there was something I wanted to talk to you about last night, but we never got the chance to really get together."

"No, we didn't. Not really."

"I was wondering . . . if you don't have anything planned for dinner, how about coming over? We can make an evening of it."

"Shelly's gone."

"Gone? Well, leave her a note to come over later."

I took another sip of water. "She left me this morning, Ruskin."

There was complete silence on the line, as if Ruskin had placed his hand over the mouthpiece. Finally: "Want to talk about it?"

"No, not really." I smiled. "It doesn't matter. But I'd like very much to come over."

"Good," he said soothingly. "We have a lot to talk about, you and I."

"Fine. I'll be over in a minute."

I took a shower first, letting the scalding water drum against my upturned face. Really, it was good that Shelly was gone. It gave a weightier heft to the feeling that I had become really and truly free. And as to exactly what had happened when I was choking her . . . Ruskin would help me to understand. He would explain.

Yes, I would come to know myself, and my friend would point the way.

Fifteen

The sun was red and low on the horizon when I knocked on the Marshes' front door. Sybil answered. "Why, hello, Charles. Come on in."

Her smile contained no hint of any intimacy having passed between us. She had a two-pronged fork in one hand and wore an apron that said: *For this I spent four years in college?*

I followed her down the hallway, which was redolent of some spicy stew. Sybil looked every inch the suburban housewife, brisk, busy, happy in her home. As we passed the kitchen, I saw she'd been hard at work indeed. On top of the stove were saucepans and skillets and a big old cast-iron kettle. The center island was piled high with opened containers, bright utensils, and several cookbooks. The microwave hummed smoothly.

Sybil opened the door to Ruskin's study. "I'll just leave you two to your man-talk."

"Thanks."

Ruskin got out of his chair, smiling. His grip was sure and comfortable, and it seemed to transmit a certain quality, a certain strength of character that flowed warmly up my arm and into my chest. "I'm glad I came over," I said truthfully. "I really needed to see you."

"Of course. It's always a pleasure talking to you, Charles. But first . . ."

He waved me to a chair. I saw that the cocaine implements had been laid out, the little rows of white powder already neatly arranged. Ruskin handed me the straw. I leaned over the little mirror and snucked in one line, then another. Ruskin took his turn.

"Hope you like this," Ruskin said. "It's my emergency supply."

I took the straw again. "Emergency?"

"This is synthetic, you see. Not quite as good as the natural kind, but"—he paused while I consumed a line—"it does the job nonetheless. Friend of mine makes it. He's a chemical engineer with DuPont."

I smiled as I handed over the straw. "And, I suppose, a member of the Society?"

Ruskin grinned as he made another line disappear. He rubbed his nose. "Yes, he's a member, Charles. Whips up a batch now and then for the club. Here." He gave me the straw and indicated I should finish the last two lines. While I was doing this, he opened a desk drawer and withdrew a thin marijuana cigarette.

"Ready for the second course?"

"Sure." Tendrils of pleasure were already beginning to wrap themselves around my body, as if I were drawing on a cocoon. "That seems like it'd hit the spot."

Ruskin picked up a heavy coffee table lighter and pressed a button that made a perfect little flame appear. "It's a Thai stick, Charles. Laced with opium. Why don't you get yourself a beer? This goes down kind of rough."

I opened the refrigerator and took out a cold aluminum can while Ruskin sucked at the reefer.

We worked it down to a tiny stub, each inhalation making my limbs feel warm and heavy and sweet. Ruskin handed over another Thai stick, and when I pressed the button on the lighter the flame seemed unusually vivid, sparkling with its own little crystalline highlights.

We smoked it down slowly, smiling at each other as we passed the stick to and fro. Time stretched out like a piece of taffy, pulling and lengthening until it snapped apart and became entirely irrelevant.

"Know what I'd like to do?" Ruskin's words came out silkily, like a caress.

I smiled as I shook my head.

"Talk, Charles. Really . . . talk." He took a leisurely drag, then let the heavy smoke drift from his nose. "I think there can be nothing more beautiful than two minds coming to know one another."

I felt a small rush of pleasure. "So do I, Ruskin. Very much so."

His grin was slow in coming, but when it was there it was like a ray of warm sunlight. "Then shall we?"

I did not have to say yes. I knew the look I gave communicated all, as if between lovers.

"Come on," he said, "I've got a pair of spare trunks in the bedroom. Let's go out to the Jacuzzi."

I moved as if the atmosphere were made of thick molasses. Once I stumbled as I got into the swimsuit, but Ruskin steadied me. We picked up some towels, fresh beers, another Thai stick, and went out.

There were high, wispy clouds crossing the sky in long, thick bands. On the side facing west they were a startling bright orange; on the other a dark purple.

We eased ourselves into the churning water. It was hot, and the whirring pressure of waterjets was wonderfully soothing. I took a sip of beer and it had no taste. I felt its coldness slide down my throat and coil in my belly.

Ruskin carefully dried his hands with a towel, then went about the business of lighting another Thai stick. I dried my hands and took the lighted joint. The foam bubbled around us like a churning ocean.

I felt more stoned than I ever had on any pot, yet my senses were as sharp and precise as a well-stropped razor. I puffed on the stick contentedly, thinking that there was no place on earth where I would rather be.

Ruskin eased his back against the rim, sighing with pleasure. He sipped his beer, the aluminum bottom of the can a bright thing that dripped molten silver. He wiped his mouth slowly. "When I'm high like this, I like to think I'm in a special kind of spaceship." He grinned briefly. "Like that one Carl Sagan used in *Cosmos*—the Ship of the Imagination." He looked at the churning foam thoughtfully. "I like to think that this Jacuzzi is the bridge, and everything is controlled by underwater switches you can work but can't see. You go wherever the accident of your fingers takes you." He leaned his head back. "What does that sky remind you of, Charles? The view from Titan with Saturn on the rise?"

I looked at Ruskin and smiled. Yes, he would be one to let his mind drift in an imaginary spaceship. I remembered he had told me how he'd driven his F-105 to such an extreme altitude that the sky had actually darkened . . . and had cursed when the controls became sluggish and unresponsive, the tiny voice of the ground controller nagging him to come back down. I smiled.

I eased my head back and stared up into the vivid, pulsating sky. A long plume of marijuana smoke drifted from my mouth and floated overhead.

And as for me . . . I closed my eyes and thought of the U.S.S. *Groves*, of the way the horizon slowly rocked as the destroyer nosed through an easy sea. I thought of the charthouse, which I always visited prior to assuming the watch on the bridge. There I would study the course the navigator had laid across the huge nautical chart, carefully noting the penciled bearings to dangerous reefs and shoals, the dead-reckoned times when the ship would change its heading.

Ah, but the chart before me now was different. It was clean and unmarked, and it was I who would plot the course. There were no obstructions. No rocks, no shoals, no beacons that indicated danger. I could go wherever I might, wherever I pleased, wherever I cared to lay down my pencil and push it along the edge of the ruler.

I opened my eyes and saw that the clouds were fast losing their color. Darkness was almost upon us—but it was more than a change in light. It seemed as if the dark were liquid, spilling onto the bushes and wooden Jacuzzi deck, pouring over everything like a thick, viscous goo. I watched it touch Ruskin's face, then slide over his eyes. The underside of his face was lit by the Jacuzzi's underwater lights, bright blue-green.

The water churned in slow motion, each bubble surfacing and leaving an after-image that was mixed up with the fresh bubbles. Like billions of tiny lives, having their moment of being, then quickly shoved aside. And all them thinking, *Is this all? So soon?*

Ruskin broke my reverie: "Ah, just in time."

Mark was coming toward us, bearing two cans of beer wet with condensation. He leaned over the Jacuzzi, his face bathed in the bluish-green light. His eyes shone as if there were two pencil flashlights in his head, tinted bright green.

"Mom said to bring these out."

"She's a mind reader." Ruskin smiled with fatherly affection. I said thanks as I took my Coors. Mark rushed back to the house.

The stars were fully out, silvery liquid drops dangling from a velvet canopy. My arms were splayed on the lip of the tub. I was perfectly relaxed, yet underneath it all, excited and thrilled. I was ready now to talk. I looked at Ruskin's wide and friendly face.

"You're a very happy man, aren't you, Ruskin?"

"Oh, yes. Very content." He took one last hit off the Thai stick. "But it wasn't always so, Charles. I was just like anyone else, I guess. Unhappy. Confused. Angry at something I couldn't really name. It used to distress me, the way I felt that I was . . ."

He let the words trail off, face puzzled as he searched for the right words. I spoke up. "That you were wasting your time?"

His smile was appreciative. "Yes, Charles. That's exactly so. I thought I had found an answer in the Air Force, but the percentage of time you spend flying is very low in comparison with what you do in terms of paperwork and other military bullshit, as I'm sure you can appreciate."

"Of course. I always enjoyed ship handling, but a Navy officer spends precious little time doing that."

He nodded. "So after I got out of the service, I took pleasure and meaning where I could find it. Isolated episodes of enjoyment, if you will. But there was nothing that gave my life purpose, no central underlying philosophy that would make me content with who I was and what I wanted."

"But things must have changed."

"Yes, they did. And I have the Society of Friends to thank for that."

"Ah . . ."

"And you shall be a member, Charles." He sat up straight and leaned toward me. "If you . . . want it, that is. Do you?"

It was really happening, I thought. At last. At long last. "Oh yes, Ruskin. Yes, of course. I would be honored. In the deepest sense of the word, I would be honored."

He smiled. "Don't you have any questions?"

"Just . . . that you tell me their philosophy. That's all I want to know. Your secret."

He relaxed again, leaning back against the tub's lip. "Charles, let me ask you what you think it is."

There was a moment of silence as I thought.

"The other day," I began, "we were talking about what it would be like if one were to know oneself completely."

"Yes."

"And do you, Ruskin? Do you know who you really are?"

The blue-green lighting twisted as his face muscles slid into a grin. "I think so, Charles. I really think I do." He regarded me steadily, the shadows covering his eyes as effectively as sunglasses.

"That night the Mexican was killed," I said quietly, "the night you came up out of the valley . . . there weren't three men torturing that alien, were there? It was just you, wasn't it? You killed him, didn't you?"

His Cheshire grin grew bigger. "And what would you say if I did, Charles?"

From far, far away came the barely audible howl of a lonesome coyote. I thought of the way Shelly's eyes had bulged from their sockets as my hands tightened on her throat.

"What was it like?" I asked, quietly. So quietly. "You can tell me, Ruskin. Tell me all about it."

In slow motion I watched Ruskin lift his hands from the water, and he stared at them as if entranced by what he saw. And for a moment, I did indeed have the sensation that I was on a spaceship, that Ruskin and I were alone in the galactic void, billions of light years from any reference point.

"Charles, it's . . . it's the most intense thing I've ever known." His words were slow and measured, as if each syllable had its own weight. "Every part of it makes me feel so alive that I could fairly burst. The stalking. The struggle." His voice dropped low. "The taking. Most of all, the taking." He looked at me, the blue-green lighting shifting across his half-darkened face. The Jacuzzi pumps whirred comfortingly, the water sizzled. "But that is not all. The most exquisite sensation comes in realizing its totality . . . and in the sharing."

He got up slowly, until at last he was standing upright, rivulets cascading off his chest like sparkling jewels. He offered me his hand. "Come, Charles. You asked me to tell you what the Society's philosophy is. I can do better than that. I will show you. Come with me . . . my brother."

I took his hand, and as I was helped to my feet I felt a rush of almost unbearable warmth. Ruskin and I were one now, united on a plane of perfect understanding. My unhappiness had come to an end. A new world was opening, as surely as if Ruskin had taken thick bandages from my eyes. We looked at each other and I kept thinking that this was indeed a spaceship, that we were the only two people in the entire universe. I thought that if he were to embrace me I would take him into my arms gladly . . . and more.

He helped me out of the tub and I could feel my heart slowly pumping, pushing the thick fluid throughout my veins. We walked to the house together, went into his study, and changed wordlessly. Then to a dining room where candles danced and twisted, their flames broken down into a thousand different colors.

A white tablecloth was set. Mark and Sybil turned to me, faces bright in the flickering light. The paintings on the wall were no longer pictures, but a dripping mass of oily pigments. I stared at the thing on the table, stared at it so fixedly it seemed I might never tear my eyes away, that I had indeed fallen into an endless void.

Ruskin was at my side, pressing a small knife in my hand. "Join us," he whispered. "Be one with us. Know what it is be a member of our sacred brotherhood."

"Ruskin," I said slowly, "It's . . . it's . . ."

"Yes, you know her." He turned to give it his full admiration, eyes glimmering in the candlelight. "It's Angela. Dear sweet Angela. And far more ravishing than in life, wouldn't you say?" He put his arm around my shoulders and smiled. "Her beauty gave me great pleasure when she was alive. But it was nothing compared to the way I—we—shall come to know her now."

Shadows worked against the walls so that they seemed alive and writhing, like gently billowing drapes.

"Ruskin, you . . ." My words came out flat and unhurried, like cool, smooth marble. "This is what happened to Debbie Hartfellen too, isn't it?"

"Why, yes." He had one eyebrow raised. "Don't tell me you didn't suspect."

"But that letter . . ."

He smiled. "A little subterfuge to throw off her parents. I had her write that letter and I drove up to Los Angeles to post it myself."

"And Vicki? Did you have her write a letter, too?"

He took his arm from my shoulder and moved to the table, picking up another small knife. "Yes, I had her write a letter. A . . . colleague of mine mailed it for me so there would be an Indiana postmark." He sighed. "These things can get complicated."

"You see," Sybil said, moving to face me, "when we first moved here we thought those illegal aliens would be a convenient supply, but it's just not the same." She shivered. "Worthless, really. All greasy and foul."

Ruskin gave her a sidelong glance. "Oh, I don't know about that."

Sybil looked at her husband and began giggling, but Ruskin gave her such a stern look that she stopped as if she suddenly realized she were in a church. Ruskin came back to me, his face floating up to hover near mine. He smiled. Reflected candlelight shone clearly in his blue irises. "Look, Charles. There will be time enough for talk later. I'll tell you all about Debbie and Vicki, and all the others too, if that's what you want. But now you should devote yourself fully to this occasion. The first time is so important. I want it to be so very special for you, as it was for me. Even though it was so long ago, I can still remember it as if it were yesterday." He waved his hand toward Angela in a gesture of offering. "Look at her, Charles. A perfect feast. Remember how she said she was a vegetarian? They're always the best. Tender, with a slight piquance that's far from unpleasant. Come."

Ruskin and his family moved to the carcass, their faces avid in the yellowish light. Ruskin began sawing off a piece, and Mark and Sybil took this as their signal to join in.

Ruskin looked at me. "Come on, Charles." The barest note of impatience had crept into his voice. "It's not very good when it's cold. Join us."

I looked down at my knife. It was unlike any I had ever seen—small, exceedingly sharp, the slender blade gracefully curved to a pinprick point. The handle was of heavy silver, intricately worked with a delicate pattern.

I wasn't very hungry. In fact, I had hardly any appetite at all.

But I partook.

Sixteen

Monday. Beginning of the week. Time to go to work. I got in the Mazda and went through the familiar stoplights, took the right off-ramps. I had done it so many times it required no thought. I pulled into Aerotel's underground parking garage and found my usual spot.

I stepped off the elevator. Things seemed strange, as if I were walking two feet off the ground, yet if I kept my legs moving somehow I managed to go forward. Maybe there had been too much to drink last night (*yes, that's it*). I walked across Aerotel's main bullpen, the surrounding desks flittering by and strangely elongated, as if I were looking through a fish-eye lens.

I went into my office and Jim smiled brightly, then puzzlement creased his unlined brow. He returned to his flowchart, embarrassed.

I looked out at the spectacular view, out at the city and harbor so far below. I imagined myself walking to the window where my atoms would momentarily disengage themselves so that I might permeate through the glass, and then I would stretch out my arms and float over the city, slowly, like a cloud, detached . . .

"Mr. Ripley? Mr. Ripley?"

I turned to the voice and it was a young brunette, one of the (*vicki, like vicki*) pool secretaries, leaning in the door. "Mr. Ripley, Mr. Anderson said for you to come to his office as soon as you got in."

I nodded and the girl left. I went where I was summoned. Anderson looked up as I walked in, eyebrows rising a quarter-inch as I plopped myself in the supplicant's chair.

"Glad to see you could make it," he said loftily, like a snotty vice-principal. His eyes rolled toward the wall clock and I saw that it was, well, so what if was ten? What did *that* matter?

I looked at him coldly. "Don't tell me I've been called in here for a lecture on punctuality."

Anderson was surprised enough to let his mouth hang open. He actually sputtered, but he slowly regained his composure, as if deciding the chew-out tactic might not work. He looked at me thoughtfully.

"Listen, Charles. I've been meaning to talk to you, but . . ." He searched for words, leaning on the cluttered desk and clasping his hands in concentration. ". . . Well, is something bothering you? Something wrong at home?"

I wondered what it would be like to put my hands around the little fuck's throat and choke the life out of him. He licked his lips nervously.

"I mean, well, aside from your performance of late . . ." He looked at me pleadingly. "Hell, man. You haven't even *shaved* today. You look awful. I think you need some kind of help."

That did it. How could I bear another moment with this bald-headed turd? Now really.

I got up and left the office, his old-womanish calls trailing in my wake. I walked hurriedly across the bullpen and punched the elevator button. Fuck it. Fuck all this shit.

I walked outside and the sun was hot against my face. I turned and looked up at the building, a twenty-five-story hunk of mirrored glass. It is nothing. Nothing but an anchor that had once held me down. But no more. I was free at last. Free of everything that had always held me back.

I went home, driving quickly. I kept checking the rearview mirror. There was, yes, there was someone following. In an old red Volkswagen. Son of a bitch. I stepped hard on the accelerator and the RX-7 surged ahead. Eighty. Ninety. An exit up ahead. The tires squealed as I took the unfamiliar off-ramp. Hands full with twisting the wheel; no time to check the mirror. I kept the accelerator down.

A wide street stretched before me. I saw a right up ahead and took it. Swung into a residential area, all shady trees and small homes. The speedometer needle blocked out the middle zero in 100. Check in the mirror. Nothing. *Hah!* But not for long. I took another turn, spinning the wheel hard. The rear end fishtailed around, slewing into a big Pontiac parked at the curb. There was a jarring *bang* and the RX-7 rebounded away. In the mirror I saw the bright plastic shards of my brakelights tumbling in the road. Up ahead some children were in the street, playing with a soccer ball. They saw me, and man, did they get out of the way. The soccer ball smacked against the upper part of the windshield, starring it.

I took another turn and slowed to fifty. Nothing in the mirror. Another set of turns and I eased on down to the speed limit. Check in the mirror. Still nothing.

I forced myself to drive home slowly. I twisted in the seat, feeling as if I were covered with itching powder. *How I longed to get out of this stupid little car!* I finally nosed into Mesa Vista Estates, and was unexpectedly taken with a new panic. I felt sure my house would no longer be there, that it had been completely swallowed up by a sinkhole.

But the house was still standing, and I nearly cried with frustration as I worked the key in the front door's lock. I rushed inside. I went to the living room and turned on the television. It was "The Phil Donahue Show," and I wanted to weep with relief. *Phil Donahue*, praise God!

I watched the show avidly, and then the next one and the next. Dinnertime came and I went to the kitchen to fix dinner (*shelly shelly christ why did you why did i*) but instead returned to the living room with nothing but a full jug of Carlo Rossi Rhine Wine and a big glass.

I watched a rerun of "Hawaii Five-O," then switched to *Moonshine County Express* on HBO. The level in the wine bottle went down half a foot. I watched a rerun of "Saturday Night Live," then the tail end of "The Tonight Show" and all of "David Letterman." I laughed at all the jokes, slapping my knee often. The wine bottle emptied. I was drunk at last, and exhausted. Time for bed.

I visited the bathroom, then strolled to the bedroom, stripping off my clothes. I threw myself onto the king-size waterbed. I smacked my lips contentedly as the bed sloshed back and forth, preparing myself for sweet oblivion. My mind let go.

I saw Ruskin. I saw his jaws working slowly, like a cow, a strip of meat dangling from his mouth. His eyes were white as snow, blankly stupid, but nonetheless intent.

I raised myself to a sitting position, stomach twisting and churning. Too much wine.

I went to the bathroom and heaved it out. I washed my face, put on a bathrobe, and went into the kitchen. I filled a glass with ice and got a can of Diet Coke and headed for the living room. Turned on the TV and watched *Thunder Alley* and *The Family Way*.

Toward the middle of "CBS Morning News" I heard a thump at the door. I opened it and saw the San Diego *Union* lying on the doormat. It was light outside; the sky rose to the east. I saw the paper boy halfway down the street, tossing a paper toward the Kings' front door.

I picked it up and went to the kitchen. The top of the paper said it was Tuesday. I turned the page and looked at the grainy photographs. Trouble brewing in Chad. Cocker spaniel puppies suckled by a cat. Milton Friedman speaking from a podium.

I saw there would be a sale at the public library today and tomorrow. They were getting rid of some books that had either been read too hard or not enough. I could probably pick up some good ones dirt cheap. They would look great in my bookcase, so I decided to go. Get cleaned up and go. Buy some books, eat lunch downtown.

I went back to the bathroom, whistling now that I had a purpose. I took a long, hot shower, feeling better every second. I got out, toweled dry, wiped the mist off the mirror (*cannibal*) and got out my shaving things. I squirted some green goo in my hand and worked it against my face and it quickly lathered white. I broke out a fresh Gillette Good News and, starting just below my sideburn, brought it down. Rinse the blade clean under the tap. Now for the cheek, working against the grain so I can get it baby-smooth. In the mirror I see (*cannibal*) my eyes half-closed, intent upon the task. Rinse the blade again. Now for the other cheek, but for some strange reason I am more intent upon the reflection of my (*cannibal*) eyes, and they are blue and blank, surely unchanged, and yet I stare into them fascinated, razor poised, hot water drumming against the sink, and something goes off inside like ten sticks of dynamite and my fist slams against the mirror and it turns into a jagged spider's web and I smash it again and the shards slip free, crashing into the sink and shattering and I look down and see a thousand different reflections of . . .

It descends like a great black bird of prey, razored talons out-stretched, its scream high and piercing in the shrill whine of a doppler up-shift. I cannot hide from it. There is no place to go. I moan aloud, sinking to my knees.

Self-loathing. It is a palpable thing with its own weight and feel, like the clanking treads of a bulldozer. A sob breaks from deep within my gut, coming out like a bark, and then another and another, and I roll up in a little ball. I begin crying, and the loathing grows all the more.

I am the most detestable of all things. I am outlaw and outcast. I am pariah, now and forevermore. The kindest man in the world would spit upon me and have me burned alive.

I wipe the hair from my forehead, sobbing. There is only one answer. Only way out. There is the pistol in the bedroom, the snub-nosed .38.

It would be over in a second.

I get up and head toward the bedroom, staggering like a lost man happening upon an oasis. Stick the oily barrel in my mouth. Over in a second. Almost too good for the likes of me.

I open the night table drawer and withdraw the Colt. Flick open the cylinder; five brass case heads glint brightly, tiny primers blood red. Yes, it would be over in a second. Almost too good for the likes of me.

I look out the bedroom window that gives onto the Marsh house. I can see the frosted pane of their bathroom's small window.

The Marshes . . .

I look down at the Colt. I imagine the little pistol kicking in my hand as I pump round after round into Ruskin and Sybil and Mark. I can see myself doing it.

And something deep inside responds powerfully to that.

Around five-thirty I saw Ruskin's copper Porsche coming down the street, going a little fast. His headlights were on although there was still enough dusk to do without. The 944's tires gently squealed as he pulled into his driveway and slipped inside the garage.

I let the Levolors drop. I had been standing here for hours, yet it seemed only minutes had passed. I put my thumb on the Colt's hammer and clicked it all the way back. I turned from the window and went into the living room, then out the sliding glass door.

I hiked my leg over the backyard fence and walked toward their Jacuzzi. I wondered if they would beg for mercy. Perhaps I could get Mark and Sybil first, so Ruskin would have to watch. But then Ruskin was the strongest, so maybe it would be better to deal with him first. Well, we would see. I stepped onto their Jacuzzi deck and looked into their house.

All their lights were already on, but it was only a little brighter than the surrounding dusk. Mark was on the floor in front of the television, head propped in his hands. I could see past the bar counter and into the kitchen, where Sybil was working. I saw Ruskin come out of the bathroom that adjoined their entrance hallway, briskly drying his hands with a small towel. He went into the kitchen and hugged Sybil from behind.

The sliding glass door was unlocked. It made a rumbling noise as I pushed it along its tracks.

Mark looked up, surprised. His parents saw me a moment later. Ruskin let go of his wife and came walking into the living room. "Hello, Charles," he said heartily. "What's up?" He acted as if he hadn't noticed the pistol, although his voice was strained. He stopped a few feet away, the smile leaving his face.

I extended my arm, leveling the Colt.

"Hey, hey." Blood drained from his face. He made no move to run. "Jesus, Charles . . ."

Something hit my legs and my knees buckled. I went down, arms waving, pistol cartwheeling across the room. Mark was holding on tight, biting my leg. Then Ruskin was on top of me and I saw his fist come sailing down and the world became a black explosion swimming with white orbs.

"He's out," I heard someone say from faraway. I felt icy little fingers snake around my throat. "Now, Dad?"

"No, not yet."

Not one muscle would move, not even my eyelids, yet I could feel and hear everything. I was easily lifted, then I was over Ruskin's shoulder and watching the heels of his shiny patent leathers as he walked to the bedroom. Then I was shuffled off and when I hit the floor the wind was knocked from my lungs. I began gasping and that roused Ruskin's attention so that his fist came down again.

Consciousness returned in the form of painful constrictions around my chest, hands, feet, mouth . . .

I was securely and elaborately bound, some kind of line wrapped around my chest and legs, hands tied on my chest, placed like a corpse. A small rubber ball was in my mouth, secured with tape wound around my head. I opened my eyes a quarter-inch. I was on the floor in the master bedroom, and through the open door I could barely see the three of them in the hallway.

Sybil was saying good-bye to her menfolk. Father and son were going into Chula Vista to catch *Return of the Jedi*. I heard my name mentioned and laughter broke out, making my pores come alive with greasy beads of sweat. The front door closed and Sybil came into the bedroom.

"Ah, so you're awake. Good." She began taking off her clothes. Nude, she went into the recesses of her closet and I could hear her rummaging around. She came out, several black rubbery things in her hand. "I'd almost thrown these away. Ruskin doesn't like them anymore." She put on some kind of black leather G-string, then an elaborate brassiere of the same material. It had chrome spikes for nipples. Then a close-fitting black hood that had opened zippers over the eyes, nose, and mouth.

She came and stood over me, placing the end of a riding crop on my nose. She ran it down my chest, slowly. "It's been a long time since I've had the opportunity to discipline a naughty boy. And naughty you were, too, coming over here waving that gun around." She laughed, and even though the mouth-zipper was open the sound was garbled.

She knelt and yanked off my shoes, then took that riding crop and began working on the soles of my feet. It was unbelievably, excruciatingly painful, each whack traveling up to my brain like a jagged lightning bolt. I bit into the rubber ball, my screams weak behind the gag.

I passed out.

I came to with her astride me, gyrating her hips against mine. She had loosened some of my bonds and had taken off my pants. My hands were still tied, but they were up over my head and behind me, hooked on to a corner of the frame that supported their mattress. I was, despite myself, halfway hard, and I could hear her whispering and cooing to herself. "We're going to eat you, Charles. Yes . . . When Ruskin and Mark get back we'll quarter you up like mutton and stick you in . . ."

I don't know if she thought I was listening; it was sort of a chant, repetitive and hypnotic. She was approaching her orgasm.

My hands had been hooked on the mattress frame casually. It would be no problem to lift them free. . . . I gathered myself up for the right moment, then swung them up and off and brought both fists down on the side of her face. She fell off the bed and I rolled on top of her and grabbed the mouth-zipper and snicked it closed. She scrabbled around frantically, flailing her hands at my head. I felt for the nose-zipper, yanked it shut, sealing off her air. Her strength seemed to redouble itself. Her long fingernails clawed at my eyes. I pressed my face against her back, keeping away. It was like riding a bucking bronc. And if she dislodged me, I was dead.

Her strength was phenomenal but not quite enough to throw me off. Finally she strained like a bow being pulled to full taut, then in sudden release went utterly slack.

I felt the big artery at the neck. No pulse. She was dead. Good. *Good!*

I hobbled into the kitchen and clumsily pulled open drawers until I found what I was looking for. I put the handle of the big knife between my knees and worked the sharp blade against the lines that secured my hands. It came loose after three scrapes. I went back into the bedroom, found my pants and put them on.

Then I went into Ruskin's study and took the little Ingram off its mount. Before I loaded it I dry-fired it a few times, making sure I knew how it worked. The mechanism was fairly simple. I rummaged through his desk and found three boxes of 9mm ammo. It took ten minutes of thumb-busting work to load up the thirty-six-round magazine. The magazine's slot was in the pistol grip, and the clip slid home with an oily click. I pulled the bolt and let it snap forward, chambering the first round.

Then I sat waiting, safety off.

I went home much later, exhausted, thinking of nothing. I put the .38 back in its drawer, the only physical evidence—so far as I knew—that tied me to the Marsh house. I put the Ingram in my closet, the first thing in my life I'd ever stolen. Then I went to the living room and sat on the sofa and put my face in my hands. The sigh was long and deep, and my hands stank of gun oil.

Ruskin and Mark had come home a couple of hours after Sybil had suffocated. I heard them come in the front door and head toward the master bedroom. I waited for their grunts of surprise and consternation. I walked out of the study and stood in the bedroom doorway, Ingram at hip level. I squeezed the trigger and sprayed them both with a two-second burst, the silencer making it sound like a string of small firecrackers. The little machine gun vibrated like a buzzsaw, letting go with an amazing volume of fire. The bullets smacked into them like sledgehammer blows, taking them down abruptly. I swung the barrel to where Mark lay gasping and touched the trigger lightly. Two separate rounds slammed into him, kicking him up against the wall with a loud thump. Ruskin staggered to his feet and began lurching at me with one hand outstretched. The expression on his face was of a desperate, terrible rage. I smiled as I squeezed the trigger. The slugs made him cartwheel backward and he came to rest on his butt, back propped against the bed. He sat there, his chest bright splashes of crimson, laboring to breathe. I pointed the muzzle at his skull and squeezed the trigger. Two seconds later the magazine was empty.

The bedroom was rich with the smell of cordite. The thing was done, and yet I made no move to leave. I don't know how long I stood there. I half expected them to start moving again, to clumsily push themselves upright and begin stumbling toward me, animated by an evil so strong and pure that mere bodily death could not put an end to it.

But they didn't. And of all the things that had happened, this seemed the most incredible of all.

I rubbed my hands against my face, trying to get the circulation going. I had never felt so exhausted in my life.

I got back up and went to the kitchen, turned on the hot water and poured dishwashing soap in my palm. I washed and scrubbed, trying to get rid of the gun oil, and my hands were soon enveloped with a thick, bubbly lather.

And wondered, What now? What next?

And the days mounted upon each other and I looked upon the Marsh house as if it might provide the answer.

Then the old man had come.

Seventeen

There was a sweet, almost cloying aroma in the Fairlane's passenger compartment, but I paid it little mind. I was more intent upon reading street numbers as I drove through the pleasant neighborhood. I found the one I was looking for near the Palace of Fine Arts, only two miles from the Golden Gate.

It was a three-story mansion whose architecture resembled that of a French chateau. Fenced all around with slender iron pickets, with closed gates giving onto a curved, cobblestone driveway. A discreet brass plate read *The Society of Friends*.

I drove aimlessly, giving the Fairlane its head. I took a turn and found myself facing San Francisco Bay. A late afternoon fog was working its way in from the Pacific, already enveloping the Golden Gate's center span. I took a right, heading along the waterfront.

It wasn't that I wanted to put things off, no sir. But what would be the use of throwing myself from the rim of a volcano? Impetuosity would only breed carelessness, and carelessness disaster. I needed to think coolly and come up with a plan.

The traffic thickened and became bumper-to-bumper. Then I saw where I was—Fisherman's Wharf. I slowed to a crawl. Christ, the tourists! Last time I'd been here there hadn't been half this many. I cursed and hit the brakes as a gaggle blandly jaywalked in front of my car. What was it, three years ago when I was here last? That's right—it was just after we had lost the baby. I had brought Shelly up here to—

I concentrated on my driving, keeping to the Embarcadero. The traffic slowly lessened, and there were fewer piers with brightly painted boats for Alcatraz excursions.

Hole up, I thought. Rent a room somewhere and get some sleep. Think things over in the morning. Then drive back to the mansion for a more thorough look—no, it would be better to take a cab. Getting rid of the Fairlane was long overdue. Well, that was simple enough. Just park it somewhere and leave the keys in the ignition. Let some punk get his fingerprints on the wheel. Of course . . .

The waterfront became more industrial, with rust-streaked cargo vessels and long, squat warehouses. There had to be a rooming house somewhere, something cheap and anonymous. Take a room for the week. Yes, a week would be enough. Work out a plan that'd be diamond-perfect.

I took a right and put a block between myself and the waterfront, then pulled over and got out. A jumble of topless/bottomless dives and peep shows stretched before me, and I knew that I was somewhere in the Tenderloin.

Well, fine. This looked like it'd be just the ticket.

I found what I was looking for next to a strip lounge with a frayed leather door. The neon crackled intermittently with HOT L ST. CHRI T PHER. A smaller, hand-lettered sign said rooms were available for the day/week/month. The narrow entranceway was dark, giving onto a littered staircase. Evidently the check-in desk was one flight above.

I had cash enough for a month, surely.

I pushed open the hotel's door. Yes, I thought. A month was what I needed. A full month to think and plan and work everything out. Then I would be ready. Everything would be exactly right. To proceed any earlier would be utter foolishness.

But I couldn't just check in like this, could I? Without supplies? I needed to stock up on things, so my thinking wouldn't be interrupted.

I backed out and began walking away, my pace quickening as I searched for the neon symbols that I required. Mercifully, I didn't have to look far. The tiny store was hot and close, its wares jammed into shelves that ran from floor to ceiling. The cashier was esconced behind bulletproof glass, and it took forever to transact my business. When he finally handed over the paper bag, I hurried outside.

I quickly walked back toward the hotel, eager to get on with the business of checking in and finding my room and locking the door. I kept thinking of the gallon jug of Four Roses in the paper bag. My mouth seemed devoid of saliva.

I ducked into an alley and twisted off the top. To hell with the rigamarole of checking in. Plenty of time for that later.

"Hey, shipmate."

I was so intent the voice disoriented me. I turned to the sound, feeling both anxious and angry at the intrusion, and saw where it was coming from.

It was a man in the shadows, outlined by a frayed overcoat several sizes too big.

"Hey, shipmate, can you give me some help? A quarter, maybe? Sure, you got some spare change for your shipmate, don't you?" He shuffled toward me, and I became aware of a nauseating stench. "Maybe even a buck, eh? You can spare a buck, can't you?"

I wanted to scream at him. I wanted to knock the old rum-pot down and trample on him. My hand tightened on the neck of the Four Roses, ready to slam it across his face.

"A buck for an old shipmate." His hair was long and matted, and what teeth he had left were yellowed stumps. "Things been hard, see? You can help me out, can't you?"

He moved closer, outstretched hand trembling. Close enough to see that he really wasn't quite so old as I'd thought. No, not by a long shot. He looked, in fact . . . to be about my age.

"Maybe you got something in that bag we can share. Not much, mind you. All's I want is just a tiny little swig. Please, mister. Just a tiny little bit. I won't take much, honest."

I looked into the wino's yellowish, rheumy eyes, and found that my anger was gone. In its stead was a great emptiness, for a veil was slowly lifting, and standing there before me I could see what I was to become.

I gave him the bottle, and he took it without thanks. He put it to his lips and drank deeply, bottom raised high, Adam's apple working.

Over, I thought. My life was truly over. The only thing that surprised me was how calmly I accepted this. I watched rivulets of booze slip from the wino's mouth and trickle down the sides of his throat.

Finally, with a great sigh, he was done. "Christy Jesus, shipmate. You don't know how much I needed that." He handed me the bottle, wiping his mouth with the back of his hand. "Here you go, mister. Your turn."

I took it. The tramp did not leave, but fixed me with a friendly gaze, waiting for the moment when he could have it back.

I slowly brought the bottle up. Oh, I was damned. As damned as the inhabitants of the innermost circle of Hell. My clothes would soon become worn and shoddy, and sores would cover my body. There would be scraps from garbage cans and whiskey bought with quarters I had begged, and I would wander the alleys until I kept the inevitable appointment with a failed liver or a wild-eyed kid with a milk carton full of gasoline.

The sharp odor of whiskey wafted upward, mixed with the sourness of the wino's stench. I stared at the bottle, wondering if there could truly be oblivion.

I don't know how long I held that pose, Four Roses almost to my lips, but eventually I felt the bottle taken from my hands, and heard the sound of the wino's impatient gulping.

No, I thought. There could never be oblivion. Even in the grips of delirium I could never forget what I had done. But though the past could not be undone, might it still be possible to live the rest of my life in atonement?

Even for a moment?

I felt a nudge against my shoulder and looked at the wino. He was offering me the bottle again.

I slowly shook my head.

He looked surprised. So surprised he didn't start drinking right away. Then I found myself reaching into my back pocket and handing over my wallet. He hesitated, then took it warily. Then I gave him the change in my pocket. Then my watch. My wedding ring.

I gave him all that I had, except for the car keys.

Low clouds scud over the city, laying down a thin, wispy fog. I drive slowly, hands locked to the wheel at ten o'clock and two, carefully observing all traffic laws. There are sounds of horns echoing off buildings, tires on damp pavement . . . and something else, which at first I can't identify. Then it comes to me that it is the beating of my own heart. It is like the rolling booms of a cadence-drum beating slow time for the oarsmen of an ancient galley.

I cruise by the mansion and see that the huge windows of the main salon are ablaze. The front doors are thrown wide, and a tall, dark-suited man stands at the head of the staircase.

I continue to the end of the street, and when I see that the intersection is clear, make a U-turn and start driving back. Find a spot and park. Cut the engine and wait, observing the scene from half a block away. It is still a few minutes before sunset; the streetlights have not yet come on.

The dark-suited man keeps glancing at the other end of the street. When a black Mercedes finally appears he calls over his shoulder and three stocky young men emerge from the vestibule. I see that they are dressed in an elaborate livery that includes white turbans. They go down the steps quickly.

The Mercedes pulls into the curved driveway and stops in front of the wide staircase. One of the young men opens the passenger door and offers his hand to a slender young woman in a low-cut evening gown. The driver opens his door and walks around the front of the car, the bounce in his step belying the gray in his hair. One of the young men climbs into the car and begins to drive it away. The couple ascends the staircase arm in arm, and the tall, dark-suited man greets them in the warm light of the vestibule, kissing them briefly on each cheek.

Another car slides up, this one a DeLorean, and one of the turbaned young men lifts the passenger's gull-wing door. A couple in trendy but elegant evening clothes disembarks. Another car purrs into the driveway.

So.

I check the clips in the two magazines. Insert one into the Ingram's pistol grip, slip the other into my raincoat's oversized pocket. I have been anxious to begin, but now I find that I can wait. Yes, for this I can wait.

The gleaming cars come, passengers are discharged, and the windows of the main salon hold an increasing number of tall shadows. The digits on the dashboard clock read 7:30. The curved driveway is stacked with waiting cars. The arrivals slowly taper off, and at eight-fifteen there are no cars at all. Night has fully descended, and the fog has turned the streetlights into lonely beacons. I wait another quarter-hour, and when I see there are no more arrivals, I open my door and get out.

The night is cool and clammy. My heels make slow clicks on the wet pavement, and the sound is mixed up with the steadied thud of blood against my eardrums, as if the galley's slavemaster were beating double-time with a great mallet in each hand.

The huge, magnificent windows of the main salon are yellow slabs of light, misty and surreal in the fog. Shadows loom large against the panes, elongating and then shortening, forming and then reforming into arrangements ever more bizarre. The music grows louder as I near, and it is a waltz, the tempo measured and stately, but of a piece that I cannot identify. I hear the first swelling of laughter, and it comes at me in a gentle roll, building slowly and easily to its crest, then dissipating into a fading swash. The waltz grows ever more distinct, but infinitely more alien, and the shadows become shapes that are no longer human, but things that are vast and fantastical.

As I ascend the staircase I know that each riser brings me closer to my death. But I am firm in my resolve to do well in this, my first truly unselfish act. Indeed, as I pass through the vestibule and the assembled turn to look at me, I find that my resolution has become as hard and purposeful as the Ingram in my hands.

One second to let them drink it in. One second to let them gape and think. Time enough for surprise to change to terror, for tall glasses of champagne to slip from startled hands. And time enough, I pray, for some to look upon their sin just as I have looked upon mine.

CPSIA information can be obtained
at www.ICGtesting.com
Printed in the USA
LVHW082041081118
596442LV00009B/145/P

9 781943 910953